TEARS IN THE TRAP 2

BLAKE KARRINGTON

CHAPTER 1

All the color drained from Tiffany's face as she clenched the phone tightly in her hand. Her mouth fell open, but no words or sound came out. She had to have heard him wrong.

"Babe, are you still there? Did you hear me? My father isn't dead. He's in the hospital."

Tiffany tried again to speak, but still, no words came forth, so she cleared her throat and tried for the third time to speak. With her heart pounding, she managed to utter,

"That's great, Nasir. I'm so happy for you." She barely recognized her own voice as the lie fell off her lips. Fuck! What was she going to do now? Hassan would surely come after her for revenge. *Damn, why didn't I make sure he was dead?* She chastised herself inwardly, even though a part of her was joyful since she'd seen the video and now knew that Hassan was truly innocent. But what was she supposed to say to him after shooting him? Sorry, my fault? Would her being his daughter be enough to simply ask for forgiveness? Life had taught her that family or no family, parent or no parent, revenge was what she was probably facing. She had jumped the gun, and it was all because of her trifling ass mother.

"So baby, will you be able to pick me up tomorrow?" His voice cut into the many thoughts that were now running through her mind.

"Ye-yeah. I should be able to. Just text me your arrival time and gate information," she mumbled in a robotic tone. Tiffany's voice was void of any emotion, but she damn sure was feeling something, and it was fear.

Nasir spoke a few more words, however, Tiffany barely even comprehended them. She was still too stunned. As they were getting off the phone, Jayden entered the room and immediately frowned at the ghostly look on Tiffany's face.

"Damn, what's wrong? Yo, are you okay?! Why you looking like that?"

"He-he's not dead, he's still alive," she stammered as she looked over at her friend.

Thinking on the other night when Tiffany turned up on her doorstep completely out of it, Jayden knew just who she was referring to.

"Hassan?" she asked, asking the question anyway. She was also smart enough to know this may not be good.

Tiffany nodded, and Jayden's heart started to beat hard and fast. They both knew what kind of man Hassan was, and he wasn't the kind you wanted beef with. Jayden stepped around the large ottoman that sat in the middle of the room. She had to sit just for a moment.

"Fuck! What are you going to do?" she looked over at Tiffany.

"Jayden, I don't know." Tiffany's voice was barely a whisper as she recalled the night she thought she had narrowly escaped death and gotten the vengeance she'd been wanting for a lifetime.

"I'll see you in the afterlife," Tiffany said, wrapping one arm around him and then jamming the gun into his side.

POP! Hassan curled up, backing away from her with a confused look on his face. The bullet crashed through his ribcage, piercing his lung, before exiting out of his back. He stumbled back up against the wall, holding his side where the bullet went in. He couldn't get out any words because blood had begun to fill his lungs. Tiffany didn't want to hear anything else from him. She aimed the gun at his chest and fired again.

"That's for the times I called for you and you never came." His body slid down the wall and as Tiffany approached, she softly whispered, "Goodbye, daddy," then turned and faded into the night.

Tiffany was weak and exhausted from being kidnapped, but the adrenaline rush that she finally felt from killing Hassan helped her to make it a few blocks. She didn't have a phone on her to get an Uber or a Lyft, so she just walked until she came up on a well-lit gas station. By the time she reached the inside, her adrenaline was coming down, and Tiffany's emotions were all over the place. She looked down at her hands, and they were trembling. She licked her dry lips and locked eyes with the young, black cashier.

"My phone is dead, and I only have like $50 cash on me. Can you please use your app, if you have one, to book me an Uber or a Lyft, and I'll pay you the cash?" Her voice held a pleading tone.

Tiffany was from the hood, so in a day where a lot of people didn't keep cash, she always tried to keep some on her because when she didn't have money for a bank account, what would she need a debit card for? The clerk had mercy on the pretty young woman who looked like she had been through a lot, and she pulled out her phone.

"Sure. Where you going?"

The sense of relief that Tiffany felt was so great that she wanted to cry. "Thank you so much." She handed the clerk the money while giving her Jayden's address. She prayed to God her friend was home *and if she wasn't, then she'd just sit outside and wait all night if she had to.*

After a few moments, the clerk looked up at her with a smile. "Ren will be here in five minutes. He's an Indian guy driving a white Tesla."

Tiffany smiled, ignoring the cracking sensation in her dry lips. "Thank you so much. You have no idea how much I appreciate this."

Outside, as she waited for the Uber, Tiffany wrapped her arms around her body as if she was hugging herself. Why did she have to be born into such a fucked up existence? She was a product of rape, and her mother hated her, so neither one of her parents were shit. Because of her father's heinous act, she lived a torturous life with her mother, and she had to kill maybe the only man who could've ever loved her unconditionally, in order to feel some sense of relief. Truthfully, at that moment, she didn't even feel relieved. Rather, all it had provided was that she could indeed take someone's life, but what good was it if she was going to be fucked up after?

Tiffany hated the fact that her eyes filled with tears because neither her mother nor Hassan deserved tears from her. Now, she wished someone would do her the favor of putting a bullet in Camil. That's how badly she hated her own parents. She wished death on both of them. When Tiffany saw the Tesla pulling up, she quickly wiped her tears and walked towards the vehicle. Inside, the driver kept trying to make conversation, but she just wanted him to shut up. All she kept picturing was the shock on Hassan's face when she shot him. The memory was embedded in her brain, and she couldn't erase the image. She couldn't get to Jayden's house fast enough because that motherfucker didn't know when to shut up. His voice was like nails on a chalkboard to Tiffany. When she saw that Jayden was home, and she knew a familiar face was about to greet her, all of her emotions came rushing out, and Tiffany began to bawl as she beat on Jayden's door. When a confused Jayden opened the door, all she could do was fall into her friend's arms and cry.

Of course, Jayden wanted to know what was going on, but she didn't pry. She let Tiffany get it all out. Then, she waited while her friend took a shower before curling up in Jayden's bed and telling her everything that went down and then falling asleep.

Jayden had been prepared to never speak on that night again, but here Tiffany was, telling her that Hassan wasn't dead.

"Do you think he's mad?" she asked in a small voice, and Tiffany slowly turned her head in her direction.

"I shot the man and left him for dead. Do you think he isn't?" She began to nervously chew on her thumb nail.

"Tiffany, you are his daughter, surely that means something, right?"

Well, it didn't mean anything to me that he was my father, right?"

"It's different, Tiff, trust me. As a parent, it's just not in us to harm our children..." As the words left her mouth, Jayden knew they were the wrong ones for her friend. Tiffany had never experienced the true love of a parent, so of course, she had no idea of a parental love. Trying to clean up that last statement before Tiffany internalized it, Jayden walked over and cupped her face softly with both hands and offered a second option.

"Maybe it's just best to lay low until you can figure something out. You always have, and I know you will now."

———

Chatima walked into Hassan's hospital room with tight lips and a grim expression. She had gone through hell with the Feds all night and half of the day. Although he wasn't under arrest, they were treating him like a common criminal and making it hard for her to visit him. That wasn't the type of shit she needed when her husband was fighting for his life, but the Feds were trying to make it very clear that they were on Hassan's ass. This was just one more thing for her to have to worry about. She had been through a lot, and something told her it was going to get worse before it ever got better. When she finally arrived at his bedside, Chatima was glad to see Hassan finally awake and responsive. He had been in and out of consciousness for a few days, and she could tell his mind was still foggy.

"I'm so glad to see you awake, babe. You scared the fuck out of me," she spoke, while reaching down and grabbing his hand. Between fearing that Hassan would go to prison and now fearing that he would die, her heart couldn't take too much more.

"I'm glad to be awake, baby, and I told you, you stuck with a nigga for a long time," he replied in a groggy voice while shaking his head and lightly laughing. She lightly giggled herself before responding, "don't you ever scare me like this again. What the hell happened?" Hassan really wanted to be dreaming. Thinking about that night, he had to be wrong about what he remembered had gone down. How could it not have been SK or any of his opps? No, instead, here it was, his own fucking daughter shot him. Truthfully, had it been anyone else, Hassan would now be trying to put together shooters to scour the city, looking for vengeance, but he wasn't going that route. He was pissed, but Tiffany was his own flesh and blood. The love that entered his heart the moment he found out she was his daughter superseded any revenge he could desire. He could only imagine her childhood and the picture that Camil had painted of him.

"Baby, I asked you what happened," Chatima repeated, wanting to get to the bottom of who had nearly killed her husband.

"Maybe you want to have a seat for this one," Hassan suggested, but Chatima didn't want to sit and get comfortable. She wanted to stand right by Hassan's bedside and hear firsthand what had transpired.

He let out a deep sigh. "It's a long story, but I got word that SK had Tiffany. He kidnapped her and was trying to hold her on some ransom type shit. I just..." his voice trailed off. He wasn't ready to tell her about Tiffany being his daughter. So, he took a different approach.

"I'm thinking he snatched her up because he'd seen her with Nasir. Not really sure why he chose her and not Nasir or even Madison, but I felt that whatever happened to her was my fault, so I went to see what I could do. You know that nigga been a thorn in my fucking side any damn way, and I've been wanting that fuckboy dead. So, I pulled up and shit just went all the way left. Nigga ended up being shot and saved by the fucking Feds, of all people. Ain't that some bullshit?" He grunted from the pain that vibrated through his body when he attempted to sit up straighter.

Chatima stood in deep thought. "It's interesting that he would snatch Tiffany. It's almost like he knew."

His brows crumpled, and he looked curiously at his wife. "It's almost like he knew what?"

"That Tiffany's your daughter." She looked him square in the face without blinking.

Hassan fought to keep his emotions from showing. He was shocked and wanted to know how she knew.

"My daughter? What are you talking about?"

Chatima broke down the video that she'd seen and all the information she'd gotten on Tiffany, and he was stunned. He'd forgotten who his wife was, and she'd just reminded him just how good she really was at her job.

"So, do you think she knew this entire time that I was her

father? Like, she wasn't hanging out with Nasir because she really liked him?"

"I don't know. Those are only things that Tiffany can tell us. My thing is, why stay in our home and act comfortable around us and not say anything if she knew? I haven't said anything to Nasir about it, but he said she originally was supposed to pick him up from the airport. However, she texted him this morning and said she wasn't feeling well."

Hassan sat in deep thought. He understood why she wasn't trying to come around. It wouldn't make sense for her to.

"Yeah, we'll just have to see if Nasir can get a hold of her, and we can ask her these questions ourselves."

Chatima studied Hassan, trying to see how he felt about the news of having a second child.

"So, how do you feel about that? You have a daughter you didn't know about. A daughter whose mother is trying to have you put away for rape."

Hassan growled. "You know I didn't rape that bitter bitch. She's just mad that a nigga never wanted her. She never told me she was pregnant. That's the shit that's shocking, but on the real, it's not Tiffany's fault. She's mine, and I've missed a big chunk of her life."

"Well, it's a good thing Nasir isn't your biological son, or that situation would've been weird as hell since lying ass bitches want to hide kids and shit," Chatima seethed. She was far from hood, but she could go there if needed, and she was sick of Camil and her antics.

"I know right."

Camil had always been a lying manipulative bitch. He thought back to when she told him about Tiffany. He now wondered what her angle was. Could they have been working together to set him up? There were too many unanswered questions.

Chatima rubbed his hand. "Even with all of this news to process and trying to deal with all you have going on, nothing is more important than you healing and getting your rest. You can worry about everything else later."

If only she knew that was easier said than done. Hassan was determined to get to the bottom of a lot of shit — mainly, hashing things out with Tiffany. After that, the war would be on, and SK and Camil both had to fuckin' go.

CHAPTER 2

Porsha entered the apartment to a frazzled looking Camil, pacing back and forth. Her wild, shifty eyes told Porsha that her aunt had dabbled in some coke, and she glanced around the room to see if perhaps there was more. When she didn't spot any, she closed the door behind her and spoke in disappointment.

"What in the hell is wrong with you?"

"Everything went wrong. It all went to shit, and it's all that little bitch's fault," Camil hissed, confusing Porsha even more.

"Auntie, stop pacing. Damn! You're making me dizzy. Stand still and tell me what in the fuck happened."

Camil huffed and puffed as if she'd just been asked to do a hard task. Being still for her was hard at the moment for multiple reasons.

"Everything was planned out and set up nice and perfect." She trained her eyes on Porsha's face.

"SK had Tiffany's little ass kidnapped and held for

ransom. I contacted Hassan to let him know where she was as a way to distract him so SK and his boys could rob his ass blind. He was going to get Hassan's money two ways. Then, when it was all said and done, SK was going to kill Hassan, and Tiffany's ass would've been right back here begging and in need, while my ass, I mean our asses, would've been set for life. But everything went left. I mean, all the way fucking left, and I have no idea where the money, or SK, is. For all I know, the Feds may have snatched both."

A small frown formed on Porsha's face. What Camil had just said was a lot to process and take in. Porsha understood Camil was out doing her thing, but she didn't know she was making moves like that. It was like she was coming up and forgetting all about her, and she didn't like that one bit. Not only that, but Camil was one cold ass bitch. Sure, Porsha had a dislike for Tiffany and found it funny when Camil would mistreat her, but to have your own daughter kidnapped was some cold-blooded shit. In fact, just the thought sent a chill down her spine.

"What? Why are you looking at me like that?" Camil asked, suddenly feeling paranoid.

"No reason," Porsha replied slowly. "It's just fucked up you come and get me to help you when you think your nigga fucking on some other bitches. Yet, it seems like you got shit all figured out. You got a way to come up for real, and you haven't put me on to shit. Not even turn me on to one of SK's homeboys. What the fuck is that all about?"

Camil sucked her teeth. She didn't have time for Porsha to be making things about her. She waved her hand in front of her face, brushing Porsha's comment off. "SK has workers, but I don't see him running tight with niggas for real," she lied. "I don't know who's a shooter, a money maker, or just a flunky. Plus, they've seen your ass around. If they want to holla, they would have."

Really, Camil wasn't concerned with putting anyone on but herself. What Porsha had failed to understand was, if Camil could do her own daughter dirty as fuck, she'd do her dirtier. Her aunt's loyalty was to herself and herself only. And everyone around her, ended up finding that fact out in due time.

"Yeah, I'm sure," Porsha looked Camil up and down. She was getting hip to her shit, and if she wanted to be funny, then Porsha would be hilarious. "Hope you find yo' nigga," she stated with a smirk before going to the back of the apartment. If they didn't find SK and Camil went back to being broke and lonely, Porsha would be sure to show her just how fast the tables could turn.

———

Tiffany rolled her eyes when she saw that Nasir was calling her for a fifth time. Although she really cared for him, she had too many other things going on right now. Her emotions and mind were all over the place. Now, it was becoming irritating that she couldn't even ghost him in peace because he wasn't catching her hint.

"Hello?" she dryly answered the call, trying not to let her annoyance show. She was met with silence, and her heart began to race. Just as she started to end the call and block the number, a voice spoke.

"We need to meet, and I'm not taking no for an answer. I'm being released from the hospital tomorrow. As soon as I'm able to get around and be out, I'll text you a location. And showing up isn't optional either. You hear me, baby girl?"

Hassan's voice was thick with authority, and she knew he wasn't playing. Tiffany wasn't sure if she was afraid the way a daughter is afraid of her father. Or the fear one would have for their arch enemy. For all she knew, Hassan was going to lure her somewhere and torture the fuck out of her before cutting her throat.

"Okay," she replied thinking to herself, *what else could she say to him?* Charlotte was big, but it wasn't *that* big. Unless she planned to hide forever, he would certainly have her found eventually, if he really wanted. Blocking Nasir, staying inside, changing her number — none of it would stop him from one day tracking her down. Hassan ended the call and aside from a slight tinge of nervousness, she couldn't believe that she actually felt relieved. They had at least now talked. And if his true intention was to meet and kill her, at least she could finally stop feeling like she was hiding.

Tiffany now had the urge to go to the mall. Some retail therapy was sure to help. Even though she didn't need anything, just being out and about, spending money always made her feel so alive. She had grown up dreaming of being able to live like she currently was, and if it was only for a short time, she was going to enjoy every last minute of it.

Grabbing her phone and purse, she left the apartment to head to South Park Mall. On the ride over, she contemplated on if Hassan did let her live, what would she do? How would their relationship be? Would he spoil her the way he did Nasir and Madison? Did she need to apologize for almost killing him and tell him that even though she falsely accused him of rape, he had a daughter, and she needed him? Would he continue to let her be in the drug game, or would she now have to get a job? Life was just as uncertain for her as it had ever been.

Tiffany pushed thoughts of uncertainty from her mind and entered the mall, ready to do some damage. She had only been inside for thirty minutes and was headed to store number two, when she locked eyes with Nasir. Just great. She froze in her tracks, while he wasted no time coming over to her. Since the last time she thought he called her phone, it was Hassan, she had no clue how many times he'd actually been the one to reach out to her. Tiffany waited anxiously for him to approach.

"Damn, Tiff, what's good? You tell me that you can't pick me up from the airport, then you start dodging me. Did I do something to you?" He looked genuinely confused, and she felt bad. He obviously didn't know about her being the one who actually shot Hassan. She hated to try and flip shit on Nasir, but he was what she didn't need at the moment. Everything inside her wanted him to be the type of guy whose arms she could fall into and feel safe from the whole situation. She desperately yearned to have someone, anyone, who would tell her they were ready to go to war with her and over her, even if it was against their own father. Unfortunately, that wasn't who Nasir was. He wasn't a sucker or anything of that nature, but he hadn't been raised in the streets or environment where the law was blurred — even obsolete — when it came to surviving and looking out for those you loved. At one time, that was the thing she loved most about him. He was a welcomed change from the guys she grew up around in her neighborhood. Nasir's whole future was bright and livable within the social lines. And if life had dealt her a different hand, then maybe they could've lived happily ever after. Her love for him let her know she needed to get him as far away from her as possible.

"I'm sorry, Nasir, but this isn't about you. I don't know how much your parents shared, but I've been through a lot of shit recently, and I'm not about to get into all of that with you at this damn mall."

"Nah, I know you have. My mother told me about the kidnapping and Hassan trying to save you. I know he's your father, and we both know he's not my biological father, so it doesn't matter."

"But it does," she threw her hands up. "He's your stepfather. That would make you my brother by marriage, and we have a half-sister in common. Blood or not, that shit is just weird. And you say kidnapped, as if I was just in a lil' fender bender. That shit was traumatizing. I thought niggas were going to kill me. So, I'm sorry, Nasir, but I'm not in the mood to make small talk on the phone, cuddle, or fuck. I just need some time to process all this. Just give me that, please."

She was damn near begging, and Nasir decided that he wasn't going to object. Once his ego got over the blow from being ghosted, he had to admit that she was right. Tiffany was going through a lot, and so was he. He truly loved Hassan, and if the man wasn't getting shot, he was getting arrested. At one time, he felt that he and Tiffany could lean on each other, but what she clearly needed was space. He didn't have the right tools to comfort her or save her, so he was going to let her be. Nasir tipped his head at her.

"I truly understand. You be safe, Tiffany. Just call me if you need me."

"Thank you," she managed to choke out.

Tiffany didn't want to cry. She refused to cry. Nasir used to be her saving grace. He was her escape from a life of hell, but now, he was just another planet in the center of her fucked up Universe and drama. She needed a break and hated to hurt his feelings, but it was time to learn to put herself first. If it was one thing growing up with her mother had given her, it was self-preservation and the ability to be emotionally cold. The same cold that allowed her to shoot Hassan was the cold that would help her navigate through this hard, fucked up life. She couldn't let feelings and emotions cause her to get caught up and lose sight of what the main focus was. Herself. She was taking a page from the selfish ass book of Camil.

CHAPTER 3

SK sat on his cousin Don's couch fuming. He had been laying low at his house for the past week, and no matter how much time passed, he was still as pissed as the day he arrived. He had narrowly escaped death and the Feds. Those were two things he should've been celebrating but couldn't. Not when his boy, Stitches, had gotten jammed up, and a few of his other hitters were dead. He'd attempted to go to war with Hassan and had failed miserably. Now, he didn't have access to the strip club, the Feds were after him, and he'd just about lost everything. At that moment, SK was livid enough to murder a man with his bare hands.

He was now being so cautious, he'd gotten rid of his personal cell phone, because not even turning off the location would ease his mind. Only thing he now had was the old track phone he used for all things illegal. It had been blowing up with calls all day and here it was, going off again. SK unflipped it and peeped the number and saw that Camil was calling him for the fourth time. He didn't have any conversation for her at the moment. He knew that she was more than likely just worried about him, and he wasn't in the mood to sit on the phone, trying to convince her that everything was okay. What was needed now was a helluva plan, and that was something only he could come up with. Even though he had some cash stashed for emergencies, he knew soon, that wouldn't be enough. Money had a way of going even faster when you needed it most. SK was considering the hard fact that he may have to leave North Carolina and go on the run. Maybe he could go to South Carolina or Georgia to get off the last of some of the dope that was still on the streets, although that route would really take some hard work because niggas always hated clearing their bill, unless they were being fronted with more drugs. Even still, SK felt he could get back on his feet if the alphabet boys didn't pick him up first.

He had gotten word of the shooting, and he had also gotten word that he had survived. SK was tired of being second to Hassan, and he wanted the nigga dealt with. It was like that fool had nine lives, but he was going to be worse than the Grim Reaper. There would be no rest until Hassan's ass was buried six feet in the dirt. And he just might kill Tiffany's lil' ass too if he could get his hands on her. In his eyes, she could have very well been the reason that things went left that day. He didn't know for sure, but she was missing, so he knew she was also alive. That wasn't sitting well with him either. So, as soon as he was able, there would be two people on his hit list that had to go ASAP. Until he figured out what he was going to do, he didn't have too many words for Camil. In a time when he wasn't completely sure who he could trust, he knew that he could count on his damn self. That was all he needed.

SK rolled a blunt, sat back, and smoked while he came up

with a game plan. He'd continue to lay low for a bit but when he was ready to pop back out, there would be hell to pay.

———

Chatima walked into the living room and saw Hassan putting on a white Polo jacket and zipping it up.

"Where do you think you're going?" she asked, confused. Hassan was supposed to be resting. He knew if he needed anything, she or Nasir could get it. She was ready to throw a fit if this man thought he was about to get back out in them streets. It never stopped with Hassan.

"I need to run out for a quick second. I'll be back in a few hours."

Chatima shook her head, looking into Hassan's face. She could tell he wasn't one hundred percent. He was still feeling some discomfort, and she really wanted to know what was so fucking important that he had to run out. Hassan had been stressing the fuck out of her. Besides taking care of him and trying to make sure he was comfortable at all times, she was working tirelessly on his case, in an effort to keep his ass free. The weight of everything was starting to take a toll on her. She eyed her husband and wondered just how many secrets Hassan was keeping from her. Women, lies, and a few other toxic traits came with the life he lived.

"Do you care to be a little more specific? You've only been out of the hospital for two days, Hassan. Just standing there has you looking uncomfortable. You need to be resting and not out in the streets in such a vulnerable state. This would be the perfect time for someone to try you. And then what?"

Hassan lifted his head and stared down at his wife. "I'm not worried about any fuckin' body doing anything to me."

"And that's the issue!" she challenged. "You are not invincible, Hassan!"

"I'm not trying to argue with you. I have Biggs driving me. I promise to be quick and if you must know, I'm meeting with my daughter, Tiffany."

Chatima was taken aback, even though she didn't have a problem with Tiffany. There was something about Hassan saying it like that and now going to meet without discussing it, that just didn't sit right with her.

"Oh, excuse me, your daughter, and when was this meeting arranged?"

Hassan was becoming frustrated. He took a second to compose himself before answering. This time, he decided that being completely honest might not be the best course of action.

"It was just this morning."

"When? When did you talk to your daughter this morning?" she asked, putting the emphasis on the words *your* and *daughter* for the second time.

"Chatima, damn, does it really matter? She knows I'm her father, and she wants to talk. I won't be gone long. I promise. Just let me do this. I have a few questions for her, and I'm sure she has some for me."

She bit her tongue and when she didn't respond, Hassan kissed her on the cheek and walked out the door. Steadying her breathing, her thoughts went to the odd position she now found herself in. She wasn't sure why Tiffany and Hassan couldn't meet at the house. Was she tripping, or was there something really odd about this entire situation? Chatima headed to her office, feeling like it was time to get to the bottom of this. She didn't care how long or hard she had to look; she was going to find out all the dirt she could on Camil, and what was up with Tiffany. She had witnessed from day one that Tiffany's mother didn't give a damn about her, but how long had Tiffany known that Hassan was her father was the question, and was it really a coincidence that she ended up being Nasir's friend and in their lives?

Inside the car, Hassan couldn't believe that he was so anxious to be meeting with Tiffany. Being anxious made him feel too much like being afraid, and he was a grown ass man. Even though she'd grown a pair of balls and managed to shoot him, there wasn't a bone in Hassan's body that feared facing Tiffany for safety reasons. He simply couldn't believe that aside from Madison, he had another daughter. A daughter that had quite a few of his character traits, and she had his gall for sure. His driver pulled up to the small café where he was going to meet her, and Hassan low-key prayed that he wouldn't have to shoot that motherfucker up if Tiffany came at him wrong. For all he knew, she was only coming to finish the job. Hassan peeped the scene for a moment before exiting the vehicle.

His driver opened the door, and Hassan spoke up. "I'm good, Biggs. You don't have to come in. I shouldn't be more than thirty minutes or so."

"Aight, Boss," Biggs tipped his head forward.

Hassan let out a low grunt as he exited the car. His body couldn't keep taking bullets. The fact that the last one came from his daughter would never sit right with him, but it was something that he had to get over. Upon entering the small restaurant, all eyes were on him. He ignored the stares as he searched for Tiffany. Hassan was used to being the center of attention, no matter where he went. Fresh out of the hospital, still healing, and not even at his best, and he was still a showstopper. He spotted Tiffany in the back of the café, seated at a table in the corner. Hassan expected to feel some anger when he laid eyes on her, but that wasn't what he felt.

Looking into her face, he realized how much she really did look like him. But more than that, he saw a scared young woman who'd had it rough and was trying so hard to play tough, but wasn't as tough as she let on to be. Hassan headed for her table with a confident swagger, and he could smell the fear oozing off her body. He sat down and glared into her eyes.

"Good to see you, baby girl. So, you want to tell me why you tried to kill a nigga? I mean, I heard some of what you said but please elaborate."

Tiffany wanted so much to be that hardened, guarded, mean person, but now looking into his eyes and recognizing the damage she'd done to him, she couldn't be mean to Hassan.

"First, I want to apologize for what I did. It might not mean much, and I know it's fucked up, but the anger and hate I had for you came from a fucked up place. It came from being mistreated, abused, and lied to my entire life. Tiffany's eyes began to water up, and Hassan was now feeling that the choice of a public place may not have been so good because his eyes were following suit.

"My mom never hesitated once to let me know that I wasn't loved or wanted. She always made it clear that she hated me for being a reminder of you. I took my anger out on you and not her, because her ass is miserable, and that's punishment enough. But here you were, living the life of the rich and famous while I was suffering. I saw you loving Madison and even Nasir. All I could think about was why I didn't deserve that same type of love. Was what my mother said the truth? And if it was, then fuck it. I might as well live up to it. Why you didn't want me, Daddy? Please just tell me that. Am I not worthy of love? Hassan's fatherly instincts kicked in as he used all the strength he could muster up to go around the small table. Grabbing Tiffany, he pulled her tightly into his arms.

"Baby girl, you got to know that had I known you were mine, I would have been there. There's no way in the world I would've ever left you in that place with that woman. But that's all behind us, and what's important now is for you to know I love you and no matter what happened, that's not changing. You hear me, Tiffany? Hassan loosened his embrace so he could look her in her eyes. You're my daughter, baby girl, and I'm your father. If you give me the chance, I want to make up for all the years we lost. We can't go back, but we can try to make it right from this day forward."

He looked so sincere and apologetic, but Tiffany was still afraid to get her hopes up. She really didn't know what real parental love felt like. Love that would allow one to forgive over and over, no matter the offense or outcome.

"Move forward how? So, you just gonna start being a father to me now that I'm grown?"

Hassan laughed. "Baby, being out of high school doesn't make you grown. You still have a long way to go, and you still need a parent's guidance. I hate that you were raised how you were and because of it, I know you had to grow up fast, but that shit is dead. You don't have to want for shit. Whatever it is you need, I got you emotionally and financially."

Tiffany was still apprehensive of becoming too excited about Hassan's promises. "Daughter or not, I tried to take your life. So, you just gonna forgive that and be daddy dearest?"

"Yeah, I am. I need you to know and understand this now, baby girl. No matter what happens, I will always be there for you and on your side. You just have to keep it real with me and let me know what's going on, but I will always have your back, even if it's to the detriment of myself, because that's what real love is. And on my gangsta side, I respect what you did. You saw me as the reason for so much of the pain in your life, and no matter who I was, you were ready to handle your business. That's gangsta as fuck, and I know you get that shit straight from your old man," he stated proudly, shocking her. "You didn't know that your mother lied, and you attempted to set shit straight. That's exactly what I would've done. I can't be mad at that. It's just now, I can show you a better way. You know, show you how to channel that shit. I know you could be a beast out here, baby girl. Anything you want to do, you can."

Tiffany had never heard words of encouragement and belief in her like that. She sat there, processing all her thoughts and emotions, creating a silence before speaking.

"Well, as a daughter talking to her father, I have to be truthful and say college isn't in my future. I've never liked school, and I don't really know what I want to do. The only thing I feel like I'm good at is selling dope," she said boldly, and Hassan had to stop himself from smiling. She really was just like his ass. But a part of him knew he couldn't just endorse her last statement, even though he totally understood what she was telling him. There was one thing that those who'd never been in the game understood and that was the feeling and the excitement that came from it. It was as addictive as the drugs being sold.

"So, let's just say I was to give you a large sum of money for feeling guilty about my absence in your life. You'd be financially straight and wouldn't have to work for a while. You could maybe come up with some business or even get a job. You think you would still want to be out here doing that dope bullshit?"

Tiffany shrugged one shoulder. "You could maybe give me enough money to hold me over for a bit, but a while isn't always. Even if you gave me a truckload, I'd still want to make my own money. I'm real life trying to retire by the age of thirty, and I'm not trying to have to slave for these white motherfuckers for thirty years to be able to live a subpar life when I'm old as fuck."

Hassan laughed. "Damn, you sound just like me. You weren't raised by me, but you're definitely my daughter. But I want you to understand what you're asking of me as a father. And I'm stating for the record this is not what I want for you. But I also know and understand that you've been making your own decisions most of your life, so I'm gonna support you and whatever it is you decide. So, I'm asking you for the last time. What do you want to do?"

"And I'm telling you for the last time, I'm going forward with what I've started — with or without you, Pops," Tiffany responded with a large smile.

"Damn, so you really going to call me Pops like I'm some senior citizen out here?"

"Shol-is, Pops! I gotta switch it up. There's no way I'm calling you the same thing Madison and Nasir call you."

"Yeah, speaking of Nasir, that's another conversation we must have, but staying on this business shit, the truth is, the Feds are on my ass hard as hell. It could be smart for me to step back and let someone I can trust run shit. And since Chuck is no longer with us," his voice trailed off, and she got the hint.

"Chuck was an unfortunate situation, but it happens in this life we chose, and he understood that."

Hassan raised his brows. Yeah, Tiffany was something else. He shook his head at his daughter and laughed.

"Ok baby girl, I'm willing to go along with this but under one condition. You must continue the plan I already have in motion. Once the money is made and that goal is reached, promise me that we'll walk away from this thing together."

"Now, that I can promise."

Hassan smiled at Tiffany.

"Baby girl, this damn sure wasn't how I expected the day to go, but I'm pleasantly surprised."

Hassan and Tiffany spoke for the next hour about her taking over the operation. He could finally fade into the background a bit and try to get from under the radar of the Feds.

CHAPTER 4

Chatima watched Hassan get ready for bed with a slack jaw. "You did what? Are you fucking insane?" she hissed.

He had briefed her on his earlier conversation and let her know that Tiffany was stepping into his place, and it was safe to say that Chatima was not pleased.

"Chatima, let's not blow this out of proportion. Tiffany was raised differently, and there's something about being raised rough that prepares you for this life. She's not new to this, and she made it clear to me that she would do it whether I agreed or not. We may as well keep the money in the family. It creates a way to strengthen my relationship with my daughter while keeping the Feds off my back."

Chatima looked at Hassan as if he'd lost his mind.

"Are you kidding me, Hassan? She is practically a child. Your child! And you're tossing her into the dope game? I can't believe this. Would you let Madison sell your drugs?" she spat, looking Hassan up and down.

"Madison and Tiffany are two different people. As I told you before, I didn't offer the proposition; she said it was happening with or without me. We both know she doesn't need me to sell drugs.

Chatima stared at Hassan. There was a time when just seeing his sexy ass made her hot and bothered. Hassan was the man, and his bad boy criminal ways even turned her on a bit. She always knew the consequences of getting caught up with a man like him. But they were older now with kids and careers. The Feds wanted him bad as hell, and he had already been shot twice. Soon, his luck was sure to run out, and where would that leave her? A dead husband was just as bad as a husband in prison. And now, he was standing before her telling her that his newfound, teenaged daughter was going to take over his drug operation. It was the most absurd thing she had heard in a long time.

"You are not broke, Hassan. You're so far from broke; that's what's crazy. When are you going to let this drug dealing bullshit go? I spend most of my hours trying to figure out ways to make sure your black ass doesn't go to prison, and you're adding someone else to the mix when you could just sit down somewhere. This is really ridiculous."

"You're my wife, and I love you. That's why I told you what's going on, but I don't need your permission. This is going to happen with or without you. Tiffany is gangsta as hell. She's been doing a lot of stuff to surprise me, but if I don't know anything else, I know that she can handle herself. And I'll be there, guiding her along the way."

"You're determined to stress me out. Speaking of things, she's done to surprise you, do you even know if you can trust her? How do you know her mother didn't put her up to this? She could've been plotting on you this entire time."

"You saw firsthand how her mother didn't give a damn about her. I don't think Tiffany would go along with anything that Camil has going on. Can you just try and trust me? We can make this shit work, and we'll all come out on top in the end."

"I can't believe that at your age, you still believe that. There is no happy ending to this game. Why can't you just walk away with your head held high, your freedom, and all the money in your accounts?"

"This is not up for discussion, Chatima." His tone was calm, but she could tell that Hassan was irritated and pissed. She was tired of biting her tongue, however.

"Not up for discussion? Oh, I know, because that's how this marriage works. You just tell me what you're going to do, and I have to go along with it. You don't give a damn how it will affect our kids or our life. It's always been about money. Just fuck your family."

"Here we go with this bullshit," Hassan spat. "What you want to do, Chatima?" He threw his hands up in exasperation. "You want to walk away?"

"Wow." She crossed her arms across her chest and fought back tears. "You would rather me walk away from you than for you to walk away from the fucking game. I'm elated to know exactly how you feel about me. Thank you." She walked out of the room, and Hassan took a deep breath.

He didn't expect her to be excited, but damn, he hadn't expected such a huge blowout either. She hadn't spoken one lie. Hassan was money hungry, he was addicted to the game, and he didn't know how to walk away from it. He was so enthralled with the wealth and the life that came with dealing drugs, he was seemingly willing to risk his and his daughter's freedom to keep the game going. In his eyes, there was nothing wrong with that; life was all about risk. But he had faith that he and Tiffany would come out on top. Maybe he was being delusional. But he wasn't ready to walk away just yet, and Chatima was either going to stick by his side, or she was going to exit stage left, but he wasn't going to argue with her every day about it. Hassan was confident that things would start going more smoothly once he finally took care of Camil and SK. Outside of the law, they were the two biggest obstacles and once they were gone, shit would be smooth sailing. He wasn't in the mood to do a lot of talking. He could show Chatima better than he could tell her.

———

Jayden stood in shock as she took in the gleeful expression on Tiffany's face.

"You're going to do what?" She thought she heard Tiffany loud and clear, but she wasn't really sure.

"I'm going to take over his drug operation. I met up with him. He trusts me, and it's all good. We're going to get this money. I'm about to have a completely different life. *We're* going to have a completely different life," she corrected herself.

A blind man couldn't miss the excitement that Tiffany had for this new venture. This was different from the one time licks she had her friends committing. This money would be long-term, although she still had plenty of money left after having Mason and Rex rob all of Hassan's spots. Just thinking about that made her feel bad, but what could she do? She had already shockingly gotten a pass for trying to kill the man. Daughter or not, there was no way he would excuse her admitting to robbing him blind. That was one regret that

Tiffany would just have to learn to live with. And now she would have the opportunity to make him all of that back plus some. Besides, her father was a hustler. For every L he took, he knew how to get that shit right back, and one thing he wasn't hurting for was money.

"Damn. That's crazy how he just forgave you for shooting him and leaving him for dead. Hassan must really love you."

Tiffany didn't like how Jayden's comments tugged at her heart strings. She didn't want to start getting soft. She had endured the hardest times, and she came out on top. She didn't desire to have a soft spot for Hassan so soon. In her mind, she was past the age of wanting, or needing, a parent's love, affection, and approval.

"I guess. Or maybe he just wants to sit back while someone else runs the show and puts a bunch of money in his pockets." Tiffany tried to downplay the comment.

"Yeah. But he could have gotten anybody to, and I know you don't want to get your hopes up, but you may have found something good in Hassan."

Tiffany still wasn't ready to get all sentimental in front of Jayden.

"We'll see, girl. When are you going to drop that load, though? You are huge," Her eyes zeroed in on Jayden's belly, making her giggle.

"Tell me about it. I got up so many times last night to pee, I almost cried. I was tired of getting out of bed. Let me rephrase that. I was tired of rolling my big ass off the bed."

Tiffany laughed, and the subject was changed. She didn't really want to keep talking about her father. Those were emotions that she needed to process in her own time and mind.

"Do you need anything? I need to run out for a minute."

"No girl, I'm just going to get some rest."

Tiffany walked out to her car, thinking about how much life had changed. A few months ago, her own mother was letting her cousin disrespect her, and when she finally stood up for herself, Tiffany was the one who was made out to be the bad guy. She had lived with it her entire life, but she still didn't understand how a woman could birth a child and hate that child so much. It was insane.

When she and Hassan had spoken about her taking over for him, he assured her that he would have a shooter by her side at all times, and that was music to Tiffany's ears. Even if she wouldn't admit it out loud, being snatched up by SK was some traumatizing shit. In that freezer, she just kept waiting to take her last breath. At times, she honestly didn't think that she would make it out alive. Having a shooter by her side would make her feel much more secure.

Her first stop was a gas station, so she could fill up. Tiffany had barely gotten out the car before hearing someone yelling in her direction.

"Smile, don't look so mean. Are you single, beautiful?"

The male voice to her right made Tiffany abandon her thoughts and turn her head in the direction of the voice. She was in such a good mood, she ignored the corny line and had to admit that the guy eyeing her was easy on the eyes. Off the rip, she could tell that he was older than her, but she didn't mind. She suddenly thought about the fact that aside from Nasir, she didn't have much experience with guys.

"I am. I mean, single, not mean or beautiful."

"No, you definitely beautiful and I can understand you looking mean to keep these niggas off you, but you can relax now."

Tiffany looked the man over and saw that he was dressed nicely. He was a little on the short side compared to Nasir, only standing at 5'9", but the ice that he was rocking verified that he was a big boy. He had dark skin, almond- shaped eyes, and a low cut that was full of waves. He had the whitest teeth and appeared to be very well put together. His beard wasn't full and thick, but the hair on his face made her aware that he was a grown ass man.

He stepped closer to her. "My name is Amar. And since I'm single too, maybe I can take you out sometime." He peeped the fancy ass McLaren she was driving and concluded that if she didn't have a man, she must come from money.

"How old are you?" she asked curiously.

"I'm twenty-six. Is that a problem?" He could tell that he had some years on the woman in front of him, but that didn't matter because he could tell she was legal. That was all that mattered to him.

"No, that's not a problem. And I'm Tiffany."

"And how old are you, Tiffany?"

"I'm old enough," she smirked. "I'm not twenty-one, but I'm legal."

"That's good enough for me. Let me get your number."

Tiffany saw no harm in giving him her number. It was time for her to experience all her new life had to offer. Maybe it would even help to finish getting Nasir out of her system. Though she was the one who fell back from him, she still thought of him every day, and she felt bad for breaking his heart. He was off doing his thing, though. Soon, he'd be back at school, and he wouldn't be thinking about her.

"I'll be hitting you up," he promised after she gave him the number. Amar looked over at the pump once she was done filling up her tank, and he saw that she put $80 worth of gas in her vehicle. He reached in his pocket, pulled out four twenties, and passed them to her. "Just so you know, you about to be fucking with a real nigga out here. You have a nice evening, Tiffany."

She smiled at him. "Thank you."

So, that's how he was coming? Her eyes followed him all the way to a red S 500 Benz. Okay, so Mr. Amar is big boy status.

CHAPTER 5

amil was smart to keep Porsha around and remain close for times like this — the uncertain times.

Although, since dealing with SK, she hadn't really been fucking with her niece and she damn sure hadn't put her on with getting to some money. But funds had gotten low, so she was hooking Porsha up with any nigga she knew that would trick off. There was nothing men liked more than new young pussy, and she was making sure her niece charged top dollar. She had just put her on with the local weed man and made sure to instruct her to get cash and some gas for them to smoke on. Hearing a car pull up, she went to see if Jamal was dropping her back off.

Camil almost shitted a brick when she saw SK coming up the walkway. Finally, this nigga remembered where she lived, and his timing couldn't have been any better. Her rent was past due and the only money she had was coming from Porsha. She hadn't seen or heard from him in over a week, but here he was, walking up like shit was all good.

SK approached Camil's door.

"Why the fuck you peeking out the window? Who you waiting on?" he barked while snatching the door open.

"Damn, hello to you too. I was checking to see if my niece was coming." She waved her hand towards Porsha's room. "I needed a little weed to help level out my high, since I'm sitting over here stressing over yo' ass."

SK looked around the room as if he was searching for signs that someone else could be there. He was never really comfortable laying up in the projects. It was a place where everyone knew everyone, and he always felt like a sitting duck, waiting on his enemies to get the drop on him. He knew Camil and could tell that she was freshly high. When she did dabble around him, coke made her a super freak. She could suck the best dick for the longest and not get tired; and when she was on that shit, her pussy got so wet, it was insane. Just thinking about it had SK's dick starting to get hard.

"Shit, you ain't gotta stress on a nigga. I'm good," he mumbled, still looking around.

"Oh, really? How the fuck would I guess that when half of your crew is dead, and the other half are locked up? Was I just supposed to know that you got away? I can get you under pressure and shit, but damn, as hard as I've rode for you, you didn't think I, at least, deserved to know that you were okay?"

Her performance was working on SK. A part of him really believed she was worried about his safety and freedom. Although, all Camil was stressing about was if he had gotten Hassan's money.

"My bad." He pulled her into his arms. "A nigga just been beyond stressed, and I needed some time to think and put things together. This shit with Hassan has me on some other shit. I'm trying to get rid of that nigga, ASAP. I could've hit you up, though, and for that, I apologize. It's just that once shit went left, I've been in a foul ass mood, and I didn't want to take it out on you."

Now he was the one putting on a performance. He was just wanting to relieve the hard on he now had pulsating in his pants.

"Don't stress, baby. Hassan is not Superman, and he's not invincible. You'll get that nigga. It's only a matter of time."

"I hope so because I'm tired of playing with his ass. I needed that motherfucker dead like yesterday. I'm ready to take innocent bystanders with me if I have to. So, the next time I get one up on that nigga, I don't care who's with him. I'm letting my bullets spray. Goddaughter or no Goddaughter, you feel me?" Camil hearing that last statement reminded her that she still didn't know if Tiffany had survived. A part of her was hoping so, not because she loved her daughter, but because she might've been able to figure out a way to spin her in her favor since it was her who let Hassan know where Tiffany was. But first, she needed to know which side to align herself with. If SK had the money, she would be his.

"I feel you, baby, and yeah, no matter who or what, I'm with you."

Just being that close to Camil had SK ready to bust some of the tension he'd been feeling. It had been too damn long since he had a release, and maybe that was what he needed to make himself feel a little better.

"Show me how much you missed a nigga," he said in a low tone as he squeezed Camil's plump ass and started pulling down his sweatpants. Nearly on command, she dropped down to her knees and began licking and sucking his stiff dick, all while keeping full eye contact with him.

Only a few sucks in and she could tell by the way he was breathing hard and grunting loud that he was about to cum.

He must've really been backed up, she thought to herself, '*cus it normally takes a long time for him to cum from head.* This made her get really animated with her dick sucking. She moaned as she bobbed her head up and down. Camil gagged as she deep throated SK's thick tool, and a tear ran from the corner of her eye.

"Just like that. Don't stop. Don't stop," he panted and grabbed the back of her head, pushing her face deeper into his crotch. "Suck that shit, baby."

She gagged again, and he shot his thick load down her throat, swallowing up every drop.

"Damn, that was good." He continued to pant as she pulled her head back.

Camil grabbed SK's hand and led him into the bedroom for part two. She was about to remind him why he needed her in his life. She was a seasoned woman and understood the best time to question a man was after laying him out, following a porn star session. Her next court date was coming up, and if SK had failed at getting the money, she would need to switch directions. Camil was looking at a secondary plan to hopefully get Hassan to just pay her to drop the charges and go away.

———

Tiffany sat on a towel that was draped on the ground, sipping from a bottle of Henny and staring at Mason's headstone. Life had changed so drastically, it was killing her that he wasn't there with them — especially since Jayden was now carrying his child. Since she had found her father, Tiffany would always carry the guilt of Mason's death since she was the one who turned him on to robbing Hassan and Chuck. Not thinking that Chuck would figure out who it was, ended up being a terrible mistake on her part. She took another sip of the liquor before pouring the rest out on the ground for her falling comrade.

"I'm gonna take care of Jayden and the baby for you. Always. Just know that, brodie. I know you smiling down on us."

Jayden had always been right there by her side as her best friend and helped her get money. But once she had the baby, Tiffany was going to make sure she stopped, and all she'd have to do was spend time taking care of her child. She had assured her friend that if she needed anything, she had her back one hundred percent. Tiffany realized she was slightly tipsy when she stood up. And it made her wonder if she should postpone the rest of her evening. She had convinced Mack to let her have the rest of the day to herself. Hassan was adamant about her having a driver and protection, but she was on her way to meet Amar for their first date. The streets talked, and she knew very soon, her name would be ringing bells. Niggas knew she was taking over for Hassan, and that was all everyone was talking about. If Amar was anybody and he had any kind of street affiliation, he'd find out who she was soon enough. But for the moment, she felt that showing up to their date with a driver would be a little too much. After making her way back to her car, she sat for a few and pulled her thoughts together. There was still a lot of unfinished business when it came to her personnel life, but she was getting the emotional fortitude to handle whatever came her way — mainly her mother. A part of her was still open to mending whatever relationship she could salvage with Camil, especially since she was the one who sent Hassan to save her. Tiffany had no idea of what her mother's true intentions were for doing that. She really thought she had maybe struck a parental cord in Camil.

After driving for nearly half an hour, she pulled her car up to the front of the restaurant so valet could park it. Getting out, she searched the area for Amar. Tiffany had become so caught up in the street life, that doing something normal like going on a date now seemed weird to her. When she spotted Amar, she took in how handsome he looked. He walked towards her with a look on his face that let her know he liked what he saw.

"I'm a hood nigga to the core. I don't even be liking these fancy ass restaurants that give you one shrimp on a plate, garnished with some parsley and a drizzle of cocktail sauce and charge you $45 for it. But you're a woman who looks like she's used to nice things, so I had to show up and show out."

"I appreciate that but honestly, as long as the food is good, I'm good with it. As long as it's not Applebee's." Truthfully, there was a time when that Applebee's dinner would have been a gourmet meal for her, but Tiffany was growing up and maturing fast. With her newfound riches and status, she was not accepting anything less.

Amar smiled as they entered the restaurant and was immediately seated by the hostess. He looked around the restaurant like he was in fact uncomfortable. He didn't like being in rooms full of white people. He always felt like he was being stereotyped and judged. Everything one assumed about him was probably true, but he still didn't like the shit. He quickly ordered some drinks, knowing he needed to loosen the hell up. Tiffany didn't want to get fucked up and not be on point, but she felt one more drink wouldn't hurt.

"So, tell me. What does a young, beautiful woman like yourself do to be out here driving a McLaren?" He finally asked the question that had been on his mind since meeting her.

"Let's just say I come from money." Tiffany wanted to keep her business to herself for as long as possible.

"Is that right?"

"It is, and what about you? What do you do?"

"I get money, baby," he answered in a cocky tone. "I'm that nigga in these Charlotte streets."

Tiffany didn't want to hurt his feelings and laugh in his face. There was a chance that maybe he hustled meth or pills, and she wasn't aware of him. Because if he sold heroin, crack, or even weed, he was definitely at the bottom of the food chain because she had never seen his face or heard his name prior to the gas station. If he was saying he was that nigga, maybe he was truly that nigga in a different world. He didn't look like a light weight, so it could be a chance he was telling the truth. Either way, she wasn't going to stress it right now. Amar was serving his purpose in giving her a night out and getting her mind off business. So, she switched up the conversation and started a light one about Kanye West's latest antics. To her surprise, he actually offered some deep insight, and they laughed and went on, enjoying each other's company.

Tiffany was pleasantly charmed with Amar on their date, and she liked the fact that he didn't try to fuck immediately after. Their bill wasn't a small one, and most niggas would feel they were owed some pussy after spending that much on a date.

Before the two parted ways, she agreed that they would go out again soon. With her busy schedule, she couldn't promise him a specific date, but she let him know that she'd be in touch.

————

A lil' sex from Camil seemed to be just what SK needed. Busting a nut didn't make his problems go away, but it made his mood a lot better. He had nearly fallen asleep after their long love making session, but quickly got his ass up and left the projects since he was supposed to be laying low, and that definitely wasn't the place to do so. He was now back home, smoking a blunt and brainstorming again. SK was somewhat surprised that after his time away and Camil acting like she was so worried and missed him so much, that she hadn't begged him to come to his place. The more he thought on it, the more suspicious he was, but he knew now wasn't the time to stress about what Camil had going on. He didn't trust any female, but he felt when it came down to it, she would have his back. Camil had already proved that she was willing to bust her gun, sell his dope, cook it, cut it, and rob a nigga for him. To him, she was one of the realest females that he'd ever fucked with, so he would give her the benefit of the doubt. For right now, he'd just sit back, wait, and see if anything different came to the light. Until then, his main focus was getting at Hassan and getting back on his feet.

He was going to have to take it back to the old days. SK could get fronted some dope to sell, or he could kick in some doors and take the dope and hopefully, some money as well. A lot of his day ones had been either hemmed up at the club that day or killed, so he had to sit back and think hard on who he would get to pull off the caper with him. It would have to be someone he could trust and not end up putting a bullet in. SK's phone rang, and he saw that his cousin, Tone, was calling.

"Yo what up, nigga? You out?" he asked hesitantly. Last he heard, Tone got snatched up at the club.

"Hell yeah, I'm out. They didn't have probable cause to hold me. I was at the club, but I didn't have shit on me. It's kind of hard to even make a conspiracy or a RICO charge stick when my name hasn't been brought up in any cases. They don't have shit on me. I haven't even been arrested in over six years. They made me sit for a bit to see if I'd crack and tell them anything, but you know a nigga wasn't about to tell them muhfuckas shit. They didn't have a choice but to let me go."

"Damn, that's what's up," SK responded. Tone was one of his lil' shooters, but he wasn't doing it big. Any drug dealer in the city who'd ever been hemmed up wouldn't think of snitching on Tone because he was far from a heavy weight in the game. He was just one of SK's higher paid flunkies. The club wasn't in his name, no drugs or money were on his person, and he didn't even have a weapon on him at the time he was snatched up, so SK doubted the man had agreed to become an informant in exchange for his freedom. And if he had, he'd just end up a dead one. "What's on your mind?" SK hit the blunt he was holding.

"Shit, I was sitting in that cell for a little bit too long, cousin. I got two days to come up with rent money, or my black ass is getting evicted. And that's a no no. My moms already got seven heads under her roof in a three bedroom."

SK rubbed his hands together. This was exactly what he needed. A nigga on his team who was as desperate and thirsty for a come up as him. Tone was all he needed by his side and with their weapons coupled with their desperation, they were going to take some niggas' shit — starting with some of Hassan's spots.

"Say less, nigga. I'm at the crib. Pull up."

CHAPTER 6

Tiffany stepped in the house after Hassan opened the door for her. Walking towards the living room, she was glad that Nasir had gone back to school. She could feel an awkward tension in the room as Chatima exited when she entered. She did, at least, offer her a tight smile, but the greeting wasn't exactly welcoming. Tiffany looked over at Hassan with raised brows.

"You got to excuse her. We got a lot of shit going on right now. I have a meeting to get to in about an hour, and I have court coming up. You know your mother still on her bullshit, trying to have me locked up for this rape that I didn't do."

"What about the video? From what I saw, a conviction is the last thing you'll have to worry about."

"Damn. Every time I think about you seeing that video, it kind fucks with me, but I understand why Chatima sent it to you. You know I never planned on using it because whatever my or your thoughts were on Chuck, at one time, he was a standup guy and more than that, I ain't no snitch."

"Nah Pops, I get it and it's just one more thing to let me know I'm a chip off the old block," Tiffany joked.

Hassan smiled. He loved the fact that he and his daughter could have such real and open conversations, and Pops was starting to grow on him.

"Anyway, I'm definitely looking forward to getting this shit behind me and hopefully, they'll just throw this case out because it's looking like that's not the only case I'm going to have to end up fighting. Chatima got word that some secret indictments are coming down soon. So, in the event that I'm still being watched, it makes sense for you to just continue to look like Nasir's girlfriend. I want you to kind of keep your distance from me publicly, so they don't start watching you. That's definitely something we don't want or need. I've already instructed Mack to make sure no one is following him anytime he's driving you around."

"Got it," Tiffany nodded. With her upbringing, she was sure that she could survive prison, but she wasn't trying to go if she didn't have to.

"How is everything so far?"

It was Tiffany's first day on the job as the head bitch in charge of Hassan's organization. "Everything is running smoothly. Traps have been checked on, and all of the money has been picked up for the first part of the day."

Hassan smiled like the proud father he was.

"Oh yeah, I almost forgot. One of my old associates is on his way over. He used to go hard and make a lot of money. He got sent away young, around nineteen, and he just did five years. He's home and ready to get back to the money. Meatcho could always handle himself well, and he doesn't have a sucker bone in his body. I want him to kind of be your right hand. Mack is good, but I feel like you need more eyes and more security with you. We're dealing with some ruthless ass niggas out here."

Tiffany wasn't really upset at the idea of being surrounded by muscle. She had one too many close brushes with death. She couldn't get the money she was working hard for if she was dead. If Hassan trusted him and said he was cool, then he must be cool, so she was with it.

The doorbell rang, and Hassan drained the alcohol from his glass before going to answer the door.

Tiffany couldn't see from where she sat, but she heard his voice turn jolly. "What's going on, nigga? You done got swole as fuck."

"Just happy to be out that hell hole and back to freedom and the money," a deep voice declared.

Hassan and Meatcho rounded the corner, and Tiffany immediately took him in. Swole was right. Meatcho was buff as fuck. He looked like he could handle Tiffany with ease, pick her up with one hand and have his way with her. Her eyes widened slightly at the impure thoughts suddenly running through her mind. Meatcho was 6'2" with a muscular build and toasted brown skin. His short hair was full of coarse curls, and he had piercing brown eyes. A few tattoos decorated the buff canvas that was his body.

"This is my daughter, Tiffany. You'll be working alongside her. Baby girl, this is Meatcho. I'm going to bring him up to speed, and he'll be ready to start with you bright and early tomorrow."

"Sounds good." Tiffany stood up and extended her hand out. "It's nice to meet you." She noticed how his large hand swallowed hers up. Meatcho took all of her beauty in without being disrespectful to Hassan.

"The pleasure's all mine."

"Well, I'll let you two catch up." Before leaving out,

Tiffany got one more good look at Meatcho, and she was already feeling safer than ever.

————

After Tiffany left the house, Chatima walked back into the living room. "Are you ready?" she asked in a flat tone, totally ignoring Meatcho. She was ready to go with him to meet his other lawyer, Thomas.

"Hey bro, give us a moment," Hassan instructed Meatcho. Once he was out of view, he turned back towards his wife.

"Why would you do some rude shit like that? You didn't have to walk out of the room when Tiffany came in earlier either. That was rude as fuck."

Chatima kissed her teeth. "I don't have anything against Tiffany, and I know you know that. I'm just not feeling this situation, and I'm not condoning it. You still don't even fully know if you can trust her. Did you ask her about doing a DNA test?" There was just something in Chatima's gut telling her that Tiffany wasn't exactly the person she portrayed herself to be. That was unsettling for Chatima. It was a natural instinct for her to want to protect her family.

"I'm good on this conversation. She's my daughter! We don't need a DNA test. She told me everything, and we're good.

"Well, if y'all are good, then why not do the test to be one hundred percent sure?"

"Because we both already sure. Now are we going to speak with Thomas or not? Because this conversation is a waste of time." Hassan was tired of sounding like a broken record. He knew Chatima meant well, but he also knew there was a side of her that was jealous.

Chatima snatched her purse up with attitude, and she

headed for the door with Hassan on her heels. She felt like every attempt she made at trying to help him and their family was in vain. Hassan was stubborn as hell, and however he ended up, maybe she'd just have to live with that. The car ride was tense and silent because she was fuming and so was Hassan, but her anger about Tiffany had subsided. She was now mad that it seemed Hassan had more loyalty for the streets than his family. All he had to do was give up Torres, and he could serve as little as five years, which was a sweet deal with a man of Hassan's stature, but he wasn't trying to fold. The thought of him being gone even for five years, made Chatima's stomach feel as if it was in knots, so she couldn't fathom him being gone longer than that.

Inside Thomas's office, Thomas could tell from the tight expression on Hassan's face that the man wasn't thrilled to be there. He decided to get right down to business. He had the feeling if he wasted too much time, Hassan would leave without hearing him out.

"Your wife has been working tirelessly on your case, but sometimes, even the best lawyers can't perform miracles. There is too much circumstantial evidence stacked against you, and the Feds are working just as hard to build a case against you. Just with conspiratorial evidence, you looking at least fifteen years in prison, and that's if the judge is in a good mood. What they also know is that Torres is the big fish they want. If they get Torres, he'll be facing a few life sentences, and that's enough for them to offer you a sweet plea deal. In exchange, you can't get away with complete immunity, but the DA will be willing to offer you five years. That's the lowest he could go. And I'm sure we can arrange for you to keep most of the money you have in accounts, as well as the real estate you currently own."

"What makes you, or them, think I can give you Torres?"

Hassan asked seriously and calmly. He didn't care what kind of evidence they had, he'd never sit in the presence of any legal representative and admit to being a drug dealer.

Thomas chuckled softly. He expected Hassan to play this game. "I'm simply letting you know that if by chance you could turn over Torres, it would work greatly in your favor."

"Well, I can't turn over shit. If I did know this Torres nigga, you think doing five years in prison is better than being dead, 'cus that's what I'd be. Dead. You don't snitch on man like that and live to tell the story. If they can build enough of a case against me to get me fifteen years in prison, then I'll just have to do that time with my head held high. Above ground. But I'm not signing my death certificate to do the Fed's job for them," he stated adamantly, and Thomas knew that to say anything else, he'd be wasting his breath and his time, so he simply nodded.

Chatima left out of the office fuming, and Hassan was getting about tired of her attitude and in the car, he checked that shit.

"Chatima, you know I love your ass, but you're really pushing it right now. You knew exactly who I've been from day one. Scratch that. Maybe you didn't because you actually thought I raped Camil's tramp ass. But you should know better than anyone that I'm far from a snitch. I've never given you the impression that I would even consider that shit. I know you don't like the chances I took out here in the streets, but I did, and you still married me. If I have to do my time, then I'll go do my time, but all this walking around with attitudes and shit every time I say something is going to stop. I have stress out in the streets; I don't need that shit at home."

Chatima bit her tongue so hard, she was surprised she didn't draw blood. She was over arguing her damn self, but how was she supposed to accept the fact that the love of her life could leave her for fifteen years?

———

The next morning, Mack showed up at his usual time to get her, and Meatcho was already in the car, waiting. He had cleaned up very nice. He was dressed in all black but even in the comfortable sweats, black hoodie, and brand new fresh out the box, black kicks, he looked damn good.

"Good morning," he spoke to her in a gruff voice that turned her on.

"Good morning," she offered him a slight smile. Meatcho was seated in the back of the SUV with her and just as she'd taken him in, he observed her as well. Tiffany looked like she belonged in college, not going to collect from trap houses. She was dressed in black, stretchy jeans, a green and red print blouse, and Gucci sneakers. The scent of her perfume filled the car, and her long weave was pushed back from her face with a Gucci headband. Her face was free of makeup, and Meatcho had to admit that she looked damn good. Out of respect for Hassan, he was going to attempt to keep his eyes to himself. He had missed too many years, and his main focus needed to be money. Although, he'd also missed a lot of pussy, and he wouldn't mind catching up on that either. The city was full of that, however, so he decided to take the focus off Tiffany and her luscious thighs. He had made a promise to himself while locked up that if he pursued a woman it would be because he saw a future with her. He was no longer going to be just fucking and giving his energy and essence to random females who weren't going to be part of his destiny.

The car ride was silent as Tiffany scrolled through her phone, and Meatcho stared out of the window. He almost questioned himself about getting caught back up with Hassan, especially when the man had been so open and honest about the Feds being on his ass. Prison was one place that Meatcho wasn't trying to go back to, but he had come home to nothing. The most foolish thing he could've done when he went away was leave his money with a female — a woman who couldn't even wait five years for him to be released, and she wasted no time running through all his cash. The money he risked his freedom for was used to fund her lifestyle while he sat in a cell with only the money Hassan placed on his books. He owed the man, and so Tiffany wasn't just a job but his debt to her father's loyalty.

They came up on the first trap, and Meatcho and Tiffany exited the car while Mack stayed inside.

Tiffany headed inside to collect the money and drop off more product.

"I'm here for the morning pickup and re-up."

"Yo, fuck that. What's up with Hassan, man?" one of the workers, Julio, asked.

Tiffany hit him with an agitated glare.

"Why are you asking about Hassan as if you can't see that I'm the one handling shit?"

"Well, can you handle the random ass bullets niggas have to keep dodging? He moved all the traps, so he wouldn't get hit again, but that doesn't stop his enemies from shooting at his workers anytime we're out in public. I damn near lost my life at The Waffle House last night 'cus Hassan out here with beef he's not handling. He's home hiding with all his workers on the front line to take the risks."

"Okay, go home then," Tiffany stared him in the eyes.

"If you can't handle this shit, and you're scared, leave the product here, and go the fuck home."

Julio felt disrespected, and it was written all over his face.

He took a step towards her, and Meatcho stepped in between the two,

"You sure you wanna do that, lil' nigga?" he glared down at Julio. He towered over the man, and Julio knew he didn't want those problems.

"Shit, I'm never scared, and she needs to watch how she talks to me. I'm not a bitch, but I'm not trying to die behind shit that doesn't have anything to do with me either," he stated grudgingly.

"Yeah, whatever," Tiffany responded. "The offer still stands. You can leave at any time."

Julio analyzed the situation and decided to let it go for another day.

Tiffany and Meatcho collected all the money, and they headed out to the car. They had three more trap houses to stop by and after that, she and Jayden had a mani-pedi appointment. Tiffany looked through her phone and saw how many people had called and texted her while she was inside, dealing with Julio's antics. She saw that she had a missed call from Amar. She made a mental note to call him back when she was done moving around for the day. She wasn't sure how she really felt about him. He didn't give her goosebumps and butterflies like she felt when she first met Nasir. Maybe that was because she wasn't a young, innocent girl anymore. Although, Meatcho did have her feeling some type of energy she had never experienced. The only way she could explain it was a mix of attraction and security. She had only been around him for a few hours, but her trust in him felt like she'd known him for a lifetime.

CHAPTER 7

Tiffany laid in her bed, trying to decide if she should hit the call button beside her mother's name. She had dreamed about her and Camil out having dinner together, laughing and joking. Truthfully, a part of her still desired a normal relationship with her mother and no matter how much she fought it and told herself it didn't exist, there was still some love left for the woman who birthed her. Not that she deserved one ounce of it, Tiffany wanted to give her another chance. Even though it took the offer of money, she was the one who went to Hassan and had she not done so, Tiffany would be dead. She figured if nothing else, she wanted to try and get Camil to drop the charges against her father before she went to court and made a fool of herself.

"Hello Camil, this is your daughter."

"I know who it is. Why has it taken you so long to call me since I'm the reason you're still alive, with your ungrateful self?" Tiffany was already regretting the decision to call. She had actually forgotten just how much of a bitch her mother really was.

"I didn't call to argue with you. We need to meet up and talk about a few things. I really want to move forward, and I'm not coming at you as an enemy, Mom, just a daughter trying to have a civil conversation with her mother." Camil sat in silence for a few seconds, trying to figure out what was running through her daughter's mind. She wasn't sure if she had somehow figured out her involvement in the whole kidnapping situation and was trying to lure her out to kill her. But the thought of Tiffany having some appreciation money for her made her suggest meeting for lunch.

"Yeah, you right. We need to talk. How about you buy your mommy some dinner?"

"Let's do it. Does around 7:00 p.m. work for you at the Cheesecake Factory? It's not far from my house."

"Yes, I'll be there."

Tiffany hung up the phone and wondered what the fuck she'd just done. Hopefully, trying to mend a relationship with her mother wouldn't backfire like it had always previously done. She didn't have a lot of time to process everything before her phone was ringing, and she saw it was Meatcho calling. A big smile came across her face as she hit accept on the screen.

"Hey, I'm out front. You ready to get this day started?"

"Yeah, I'll be right down," she excitedly responded.

———

After a busy morning of pick-ups, drop offs, and phone calls, Tiffany was famished. As if he had read her mind, Meatcho spoke up. Prior to this moment, they had only spoken when she was giving him subtle instructions. *Count the money, weigh this, hold that.* Meatcho quickly found that working with her wasn't bad. She didn't do a lot of unnecessary talking like most females, and she seemed to be about her business. She wasn't moving sloppy and reckless, and he didn't mind assisting her. Shit, this was easy ass money.

"Mind if we stop and get food?" he asked right before his stomach rumbled.

"Heck no. I'm starving, and I'm sure Mack is too. What do you have a taste for?"

"I'll let the lady decide."

Tiffany didn't miss the way his eyes roamed over her body. She also didn't miss the fact that her body heated up under his intense glare. "Um, we can do a nice burger joint. Somewhere with real beef. Not no Burger King or Wendy's type shit." She frowned her face up, and Meatcho laughed.

"I'm with you on that one, ma. I just came home from prison. I wouldn't feed a dog some of the shit they served in there. It's safe to say I mostly survived off canteen. I didn't care how hungry I got, I refused to put half that shit in my body."

"How is prison?" she asked, and he raised his eyebrows. "I mean, I know it's not a good place. But all I know is what I've seen on TV and movies. Given the life that I live, though, I can't rule out the fact that I might end up there one day."

"I want to tell you not to think like that, but there's never shit wrong with being realistic and preparing yourself for the worst. I can assure you that it's no place for a pretty lady like you. Whatever you've seen on TV and in movies, imagine worse. It's gotta be the closest thing to hell on earth."

Tiffany gave a head nod. "What made you want to come home and get right back in the game? You don't fear going back?"

"To me, the second closest thing to hell on earth is not having shit. Staying from pillar to post, not knowing where your next meal is coming from. That shit isn't a way to live either. I can't be out here with nothing. This time around, I just gotta be smart about it, though. What about you? Why you out here, taking these risks when your pops is rich as fuck, and you can just be spoon fed like his other kids?"

Tiffany chuckled. "I just really found out that Hassan was my father, so I grew up in conditions you just spoke about. We didn't really have shit and on top of that, I had a mother who didn't hesitate to let me know that she hated my existence. The home that I grew up in can't be much worse than prison. Things happened to me that made me a little less fearful and a little bolder. I don't want to go to prison, but if my childhood didn't break me, that won't either. Like you said, I can't be out here with nothing. I'm too old to just be out here, depending on Hassan too."

"Makes sense."

Mack arrived at the food spot, and they all piled out of the car. Even though Meatcho was certain that Tiffany had more money than him, he still told the cashier to add Tiffany's food to his tab. He may not have had a lot, but he was a man, and she was a woman. She wouldn't be paying for her own food in his presence. He wasn't *that* broke that he couldn't get her a burger and some fries. She turned to look at him after they ordered their food.

"You didn't have to do that. You just came home. Let me pay you your money back."

"Don't insult me, ma." Meatcho smiled at Tiffany. "I know you're the boss and all, but I'm still a gentleman. Being fresh off the yard doesn't change that. It's only $46 worth of food. I'm sure I can manage to pay for that."

Tiffany offered him a smile and stood off to the side to wait on her food. Their numbers were called, and Tiffany and Meatcho found a table in the back of the restaurant.

"You don't have a girlfriend? Nobody's gonna be beefing

about you being out with me and having to spend so much time with me?" she pried.

"No. I'm unattached. The chick I did fuck with a few times after I came home has a nigga, so she'd be doing herself a disservice by showing out behind me."

"Look at you being a homewrecker," Tiffany smirked, and Meatcho laughed.

"I'm just a nigga fresh off a five-year bid who wanted some pussy. I knew her from back in the day. She's been wanting to fuck, so who was I to deny her? Her having a nigga is her problem."

"That's one way to look at it," Tiffany stated sarcastically.

"What about you? You don't have a man?"

Tiffany's mind went to Nasir and Amar. They were the closest things to boyfriends she'd ever had. For some reason, she didn't care to tell him that she dealt with Amar. "I date casually," she shrugged. "But I don't have a boyfriend. I'm actually kind of too busy for a relationship. Sometimes, by the time I'm done for the day, I'm exhausted. I don't know too many men who'd want to come last to the streets in their relationship. Especially when it's usually them with no time for their significant other."

"You also have to deal with a nigga who would be secure in what you do. For instance, if you do deal with someone who hustles. You being higher up on the food chain and having so much more money and power, that shit could be a blow to his ego if he's not on the same level."

"I definitely get that." It was like he was psychic and telling her, her future with Amar. Tiffany could tell by the look in his eyes when she saw him at the trap that he had mixed feelings, and it wasn't just about him being shocked.

"Maybe you won't even end up with a street nigga. You might find some old square ass nigga."

"I'm not sure a square ass nigga will want any parts of my life. I need someone who understands me and can relate to what I have going on. Someone who won't cry about wanting all my time and won't be intimidated by what I have. At this point, maybe I need to date a nigga like Torres."

"There you go. That would solve your problems," Meatcho agreed, and Tiffany smiled and shook her head.

"If only it was that simple."

They finished up their meal, and Tiffany got back to work.

———

Tiffany pulled her car up to the valet station in front of Southpark Mall and handed the young, white male her keys. She quickly noticed that Camil had already arrived and was standing out front.

"Hey, Ma. I see you got here early."

"Yeah, I did, but I don't have a car worthy of valeting, so I'm parked in the garage."

Tiffany ignored the sly remark. She didn't want to aid her into creating a downward mood so instead, she kept it positive.

"That's ok. You know things can change quickly just like they did for myself."

"Well, you just remember who was a part of helping and making those things change so fast." *OK. This was a second strike,* Tiffany thought to herself but again, she reminded herself to stay upbeat. They went inside and placed their names on the waiting list and within a few minutes, were called to their table.

"Do you know what you want to eat?"

"Look Tiff, it doesn't matter. Can we just get down to what we're both here for?"

"Oh, and what is that?"

"For my compensation for saving your lil' ass. If it wasn't for me, you wouldn't be sitting in this fancy restaurant or driving that expensive car, nor wearing them clothes. So please don't sit your lil' ass over there like you're doing something for me, or that you're somehow better, because you're not."

"Wow, I guess this was really a bad decision. Here I was, trying to extend an olive branch to you for a fucked up childhood and maybe build a relationship moving forward, since I'm an adult now. But I see nothing's changed with you. You will always be a self-centered, money hungry bitch. So just tell me what the fuck it'll take for your miserable ass to drop the charges against my father. It's not a case you can win anyway."

"Ohhhh, so now he's your father. Where was he when this miserable bitch was the one taking care of your lil' red ass? That rapist of a father was nowhere around, and now you sit here, trying to negotiate for him?"

"Ma, we both know he didn't rape you, so let's drop the act and just name the amount."

"Who the fuck you talking to like that? I'm still your mother and you calling me a liar because you and that no good nigga have been somewhere plotting against me."

The waiter came over and Tiffany waved him off. She was really regretting this attempt at being civilized with Camil and was now wondering what was going through her mind when she chose a public place to do so. She wanted to tell her to drop the victim act because she had seen the video but knew she couldn't expose Hassan's trump card if her mother wouldn't do the right thing.

"Camil, I'm asking you for the last time, what do you want? I'm prepared to give you twenty-five thousand now and another twenty-five after the case is dropped and some paperwork is signed."

"Hahahaha! If you think I'm taking that lil' ass money, you and that rapist is crazy as fuck. It's going to take at least two hundred and fifty thousand."

Realizing that there was no way she was going to be able to reason with her mother, Tiffany reached into her purse and grabbed two one-hundred-dollar bills and placed them on the table.

"Order whatever you want and have a great life, Camil."

―――――

That Monday, Darnell Johnson, AKA Hassan, walked into court looking like the millionaire he was. The tailored suit that he wore cost more than the monthly salaries of all the federal agents gawking at him. Hassan entered the courtroom like the G he was with Chatima by his side and Tiffany behind him. When he entered the courtroom, Camil turned around and looked over her shoulder, and her face turned red upon seeing Hassan and Tiffany. She saw now that her daughter had obviously abandoned her and was really riding with this nigga. Camil glared at Tiffany with a frown on her face as she took in the girl's designer threads. Her eyes stopped down at Tiffany's Louboutin-clad feet, and her blood boiled with jealousy and anger. Hassan had taken her ass in and upgraded her in a major way. The slight come up that Camil thought she had was put on pause since SK was trying to get back on his feet. He had been running around town on his jack boy shit, and he pulled off a few capers, but it wasn't anything that put him to being close to where he needed to be. Since his pockets were touching, she had to rely on her old ways of getting money, and she didn't like it. Camil wasn't sure if she was getting soft or what, but she wasn't about to go back to suckin' dick and fuckin' niggas for a couple of dollars. Not when SK could find out and leave her ass right before he got back on his feet. Camil wasn't trying to miss that payday, so she was waiting it out. But it was hard, and Tiffany walking around like some spoiled, drug mafia princess was eating her alive.

Camil had always been jealous of Tiffany — even when they didn't seem to have much. But now that it appeared that she had Hassan's approval and new monetary blessings, Camil was even more heated.

"Your honor, we have some new evidence that I'm sure will clear my client's name and that way, we won't have to waste anymore of the court's time." Chatima's voice made Camil abandon her thoughts of jealousy towards Tiffany. She glared at Chatima, wondering what in the hell she was talking about.

"I wasn't aware of any new evidence," the DA stated lamely.

Chatima smirked. "Now, you do. It was obtained at the last second, Your Honor, but I assure you, it's relevant. It's a little graphic, but relevant. If you'd like to view the footage in private, I completely understand."

Camil's heart raced as the judge granted Chatima permission to play the tape in his chambers. She said it was graphic. What in the hell was it, and how did it pertain to her and Hassan?

"I've tried to edit the majority of the video, Your Honor because as I said, it's graphic. I felt that we simply needed to get straight to the point."

The judge's face turned beet red as Chatima pressed play, and the loud moans from the video filled the room. Hassan was fucking her savagely, and it was clear to everyone watching that Camil was enjoying herself. "Fuck me, daddy. Fuck me!" she called out on the tape, making the judge's face turn even redder.

There were a bunch of shocked faces in the room, and Camil looked like she was ready to crawl underneath her chair.

"I was videotaped without my permission!" she yelled, wanting to walk over to Hassan and put a bullet in his head.

Chatima took it upon herself to stop the video. Even though Chuck was dead, Hassan didn't want that part played in court. "The tape may have been recorded without your permission, but as everyone in this room can see, it was consensual sex and not rape. You were begging for it. So, when did he rape you? Was it this night or a different night?" Chatima asked, knowingly.

Camil was so mad, she couldn't answer. It felt like steam was shooting from her ears. That was how mad she was. Her own daughter had teamed up with her enemy, and they were conspiring against her. SK should have killed that little bitch. Camil wanted to cry, but it was out of anger. She wasn't the type of weak bitch to sit around crying while she was sad. Now more than ever, she needed a bump of coke to calm her fucking nerves. Camil sat in horror as the judge not only dismissed the case against Hassan, but stated she should have Camil locked up for lying on him. The day had been a total and complete bust, and she wasn't sure who wanted Hassan and Tiffany dead worse, her or SK.

CHAPTER 8

Camil couldn't tell SK why she was all of a sudden so livid with Hassan and Tiffany, but she wanted them wiped off the face of the earth. She was pacing back and forth, and SK looked at her strangely. "Fuck wrong with you?" he asked, pissed that he only had $175 left to his name after he copped some dope. SK was ready to get back on his feet and even though he was broke, he had product, so he knew he would shake back soon. He had just got done bagging shit up and was going to hit the streets. He didn't care if he had to hustle all night.

"Things are just different. I hate to see you stressing about money like this," she lied. "When are you going to handle Hassan? You already know I got your back. I'm down to ride if you need me; just say the word."

SK became instantly irritated. "You think I don't want that nigga? He's the reason I'm broke and all my homies are either dead or in jail. Bishop went to that nigga's crib to get him and ended up in a lake. I have to stop thinking and moving based off emotions and move smart, so I can stop wasting my time.

Let me handle this and stop trying to play me like I can't handle my shit. Fuck I look like needing you to get at Hassan?"

Camil bit her tongue. SK was already in a foul mood, and if she said what she wanted to say, he'd have a fit. It seemed that he needed her, or some damn body, to get at Hassan. That nigga was walking around like he couldn't be touched, and Camil wanted to get at him her damn self. She wasn't sure where that video came from, but it messed her up, and she wasn't happy about it. She had thick skin, and there wasn't too much that could embarrass her, but that stunt in the courtroom did it. She couldn't believe that Hassan knew about that tape all this time, and he never said anything. He let shit get this far, and he held the trump card the entire time. He could've saved her a lot of time. She just knew she was going to win the case and leave that courthouse a rich woman. She had never felt so stupid, and Camil needed some cash, and she needed it fast.

"Okay, you don't need my help to get at Hassan," she stated sarcastically. "The meal ticket was right there in Tiffany. Hassan would've paid lovely to get her back. How in the hell did that go wrong?"

"Why are we talking about old shit?" SK barked. "You think I haven't sat and thought about all the shit you just said? Fuck out my face with that bullshit. You the one over there, pacing like you done took more losses than me. Besides, this nigga done went ghost. We've been hitting all his people and still no response. So miss me with that fuck shit." She was pissing SK off, and he wasn't trying to hide it.

"All I'm fucking saying is, have you at least tried looking at one of their Instagram or Facebook accounts or something? His fucking wife is an attorney, so she's gonna have public information. Figure something out for fuck's sake." SK had to admit, he hadn't considered that method, but there was no way he was going to let her think she had just put him onto anything he hadn't already thought of.

"Like I said, I'm on it and I'm done talking about it."

Camil didn't need his attitude when she had one of her own. She left the house and stormed out to her car. She needed some air and time to come up with another plan. Camil headed home. Her mouth was watering at the thought of getting the last bit of coke she had hidden in her dresser drawer. When she walked into her apartment, she saw Porsha leaving out.

"Hey, did you buy some food? Last time I was in the kitchen, it was bare as hell in there."

Porsha sucked her teeth. "I just bought cleaning supplies and paid the internet bill. I don't live here alone."

"But you live in my apartment," Camil snaked her neck. "All you had to buy was cleaning supplies and pay the internet bill, and you bitching about that? You're going to have to come up off more than that if I put your ass out on the street."

Porsha chuckled. Now that Tiffany was gone, Camil was being a bitch towards her, and she wasn't going for that shit. "I'll be out of here by the end of the week." Porsha was already pissed that after Camil hooked up with SK, she all but abandoned her anyway. And if she hadn't followed Camil's lead, she wouldn't have been such a bitch to Tiffany. Tiffany had come up and was shitting on them all, and Porsha was regretting all the times she was mean to her. To have Camil turning on her was a slap in the face, and Camil felt hit just as hard. She was losing one of the last money sources she had, and Camil was even more pissed off and stressed out.

"You won't be out of here by the end of the day, you'll be

out of here now. Go grab all your shit and get it the fuck out my place. I'm sick of you ungrateful ass bitches. You start smelling yourselves, and then it's fuck me. Get out now." Camil was damn near foaming at the mouth.

Porsha gladly went and grabbed her things from the room in the apartment. She didn't even know where she was going to go, but she didn't care. As long as she wasn't up under evil ass Camil, it would be great. Camil stood there with her arms folded, watching Porsha grab her things. She didn't need Tiffany, she didn't need Hassan's money, she didn't need SK, and she didn't need Porsha. Camil was going to show all of them that she could come up without them. When Porsha was done collecting her things, Camil couldn't have been happier. She all but slammed the door behind Porsha, and she headed to her room to get the coke. Camil was anticipating the hit so bad, her hands were damn near shaking. When she had finally snorted the narcotic into her nostrils, she waited anxiously for that rush and when it hit her, she moaned. She could finally relax and let the shame from court melt off her. She slowly opened her glassy eyes and cleared her throat. This was what she needed to clear her mind. Now, she just had to come up with a game plan.

————

That morning, Tiffany couldn't wait to see Meatcho, so she was already downstairs waiting when he pulled up. They were doing collections in a few new spots that he'd reclaimed since being back home. He wanted his people to meet the boss so there wouldn't be any problems or confusion. Tiffany was motivating him, whether she knew it or not. Arriving at the small house near the end of the cul-de-sac, they both got out while Mack put the truck in park.

"Yo what up playboys, let me introduce y'all to the boss lady."

Inside the house were three dudes sitting in the living room, playing the Xbox, and Tiffany instantly locked eyes with the one she already knew—Amar. She couldn't miss the stunned expression that covered his face as his eyes darted from her to Meatcho. Meanwhile, she held back a smirk as she recalled the words he spoke to her about being a heavy hitter in the game. Working in one of the trap houses didn't make for a heavy hitter, but she wouldn't burst his delusional bubble. Instead, she kept it all business and saved Amar's face in front of his boys.

One of the other men stood up and headed towards the back. There was an awkward silence in the room until he came back two minutes later. "$14,500. It's all there."

She nodded as she unzipped the bag and peered inside.

"I'll be back around four. How much work is here?" Meatcho asked.

"A little more than three ounces."

"Cool. Hit me if you need more." With that, they turned heels and left the house, leaving Amar staring darts into their backs.

———

"Chatima, I told you I'm tired of talking about this! The answer is till fucking no!"

"Hassan, you wouldn't even have to take the stand. There would be no paperwork involved at all. The only ones who would even know of your involvement are you, myself, and the lead federal Prosecutor."

Chatima had spent the last hour trying to reason with her husband. The Federal attorney had come back to her with what she felt was the sweetest deal ever. They would allow Hassan to keep all his assets and serve out a seventy month sentence at a low-level camp for merely notifying them of when Torres would be on American soil. The new Federal prosecutor had set his sights on a bigger fish, which was the Colombian government, so he wanted to capture Torres on US grounds and leverage his extradition for testimony against the current regime. With this new offer, Hassan wouldn't even be involved with the case outside of letting them know when and where the meeting was to take place.

"You right. No one else would know, but I would know, and that's enough. Setting a nigga up is the same as snitching, and I couldn't live with myself. Why do you not understand that?"

"Maybe because I've seen you live with a lot of other shit, and you seem to have more commitment to the vows of the street life than to the ones of our marriage."

"Yeah, I'm not about to do this with you tonight. Can you please just call Madison down for dinner? Because if I'm about to get cooked up like you say, at least let me enjoy my time out here in the free world in peace."

Chatima shook her head in despair. There was no convincing Hassan that he needed to take this deal for himself and his family.

———

Meatcho and Tiffany sat in the waiting room of the doctor's office while Jayden was being seen by her obstetrician. It had been a long morning, but there was no way Tiffany wasn't going to make all of Jayden's appointments, just like she had promised Mason and her best friend.

"You know I really appreciate you coming inside and

waiting with me, but you could've stayed out and grabbed a nap in the car like Mack's lazy ass." They both laughed.

"Yeah, that nigga do be tired all the time. I told him it's because of all that bullshit he be eating. But you know you good people and like being around you."

"Oh, is that right? So, what makes me good people, Mr. Meatcho?"

"Well, first thing, you know how to address your elders correctly, and I appreciate that," he joked back, generating a large smile on her face. "But on the real, you're just an easy person to connect with. I like how our conversations just flow and aren't forced, and the fact that we can just sit in silence in one another's presence and not feel uncomfortable."

"Yeah, I like that too. You got to be the first man I met who doesn't have a problem with me expressing myself fully and not feeling judged like I'm being bossy or a bitch. Most of the time, I feel like I have to hold my thoughts back to guard a man's ego."

"Nah, never that, ma. I am who I am regardless of place, time, or circumstance. Plus, I learned a lot being raised by my grandparents and one thing their relationship showed me was that whoever is more qualified to handle certain things should do so. Like, my grandfather went to work every day, but at the end of the week, he brought his check home and gave it to my grandma. She handled all the bills and distributed the money. But never once did I hear her talk down or try to belittle him. When I got older, I asked him why he used to do that, and he told me he wanted her to know what we had so he didn't have to worry about her asking him for crazy shit he couldn't afford. She had all the money and the bills, so she knew exactly what he could and couldn't do."

"Wow, your grandfather is a smart man. I'd love to meet him one day."

"I would've loved that. I'm sure both of them would've loved your energy and spirit. But they both have passed."

"Oh, I'm so sorry to hear that. I know how it is to feel alone out here in this world."

"Yeah, the one thing that still haunts me is that I wasn't able to fully keep my word to my grandfather because I was locked up when my grandma died. He had asked me to take care of her on his deathbed three years prior, and two years into my bid, she got sick and passed away. That's why I know that if and when I get my family, there's nothing I'm not doing to make sure they're straight and secure."

Jayden coming out from behind the door interrupted their convo, and Meatcho stood up to go outside and wave for Mack to bring the truck around.

Once they were all inside the large SUV, Tiffany decided to check in with Hassan via text message. While she was waiting for his response, she got a text message from Amar. She was surprised that it'd taken him so long to reach out to her. It'd been hours since she saw him. Since she was always vague when he asked her what she did, Tiffany knew he had to be shocked. She sent him a quick text, letting him know that she would call him later. She'd just sent the text when she heard loud ass popping sounds. Tiffany and Jayden both ducked, while Mack jerked the truck to the left, damn near sideswiping a car. Meatcho grabbed his gun from his lap and began returning fire to the old Impala, where the gunfire continued to come from. Mack was trying to help shoot back, also while weaving in and out of traffic. He couldn't shoot and drive, so instead, he floored it and was trying to get away from the bullets as fast as he could. The vehicle began to fish-tail, and they knew that one of the bullets had more than

likely penetrated one or more of the tires. Mack had no choice but to run up on a curb as the black car whizzed past them. Someone had taken shots at them in broad daylight, but the assailants weren't smart enough to not stop and try to get out and finish the job, so they had no way of knowing who had shot at them. Mack immediately pulled out his phone and began to call Hassan while Meatcho consoled Tiffany and Jayden.

Tiffany waited for the pounding of her heart to slow down. This was the downside of the game, and the part that she could never get used to. The words she'd just spoken to Julio entered her mind, and she now understood how he felt. Something told her she was ducking bullets meant for Hassan. Or maybe they were meant for her now that she was the boss.

"Y'all good?" Mack asked as he waited on Hassan to answer.

"Yeah, we're good." Tiffany tried to appear calm and unfazed by the shooting. But the pounding of her heart wouldn't slow down. She was nervously checking all of Jayden's clothes for any sign of blood. There was no way she could live with herself if she'd just put her best friend and her unborn child's life into such danger.

"Jayden, you and my nephew good?"

"Yeah, we good. He just acting like he busting his gun back inside of me," she responded jokingly. Her humor lightened up the whole mood.

"You think this is your boy SK?" Meatcho asked Tiffany.

"Yeah, who else? I guess this is what Julio was crying about."

Mack talked to Hassan for a bit, before getting back in the

truck and waiting for someone to come pick them up. Hassan instructed him to leave the vehicle, and they would have it towed later. It wasn't ideal, but Tiffany knew business might have to slow down just a bit until SK was finally handled, and he needed to be handled fast. They had money, resources, and connections. There was no reason that they shouldn't have been able to find SK's ass. Suddenly, Tiffany had a thought. Her mother seemed to be connected to SK. She didn't know how much SK cared about her, but maybe it was worth having Camil snatched to see if that would draw SK out. Hassan needed to go ahead and lay that nigga down, and she would be there with all of his other shooters to help him if need be, but SK's bitch ass had to go. He was now getting too close to her and the ones she loved.

As soon as Tiffany was in front of Hassan, she didn't even let him speak before she told him what was up.

"I may know how we can flush SK out. Camil had some kind of connection to him. Snatch her ass up, and it might draw him out. I know her address." She stared into Hassan's eyes with conviction. Once again, he was almost shocked at the callous behavior that Tiffany could exhibit. There was nothing pussy about her for real, and that made Hassan proud.

"Let's do that shit then. Tell me where to get her ass from. She's been a thorn in my side for years any damn way."

Before Tiffany could even give him the address, Hassan's phone rang, and after he answered, Tiffany could tell from the confused look on his face that something else had happened. "Wait, Chatima, you have to slow down. I can't understand you. Calm down and tell me what's wrong."

Hassan stood up because even though he couldn't under-stand her, Chatima was too hysterical for his liking. Some-thing was wrong, and he was willing to bet that it had SK's

name all over it. "You said what?" His face turned red, and Tiffany knew something was up. Hassan took the phone away from his ear and looked at the screen. "Hold on, Chatima," he barked. "Yo!" he yelled after switching over.

"Yeah, I got your daughter, nigga," SK taunted.

CHAPTER 9

Tiffany, Hassan, Mack, and Meatcho dipped down in the old Honda Civic hooptie, as Camil exited her house and jumped in the car.

"Make sure you hang back, Mack," Hassan instructed.

"Yeah, we don't want to spook the bitch," Meatcho added. They were hoping that Camil would lead them to SK's sucker ass. Hassan was planning on murdering everyone involved if anything happened to Madison. It was a short ride when Camil turned into the parking lot of a small trailer park off North Tryon Street.

Camil switched her hips up to the door of the small, white mobile home and knocked on the door. One of SK's henchmen opened the door and let her in. Camil stepped further into the room, and she saw a scared young girl, looking terrified. She was tied to a chair and had a gag in her mouth, so she couldn't scream. Camil had an idea of who the girl was, but she didn't want to assume. "Who is this?"

"It's Hassan's daughter. And if he wants her back alive,

he's going to have to come get her ass and bring me my money and meet his maker. I'm over that hoe ass nigga."

Tears rolled down Madison's cheeks. If she made it out of that incident alive, she'd be scarred for the rest of her life. She was a suburban kid built nothing like Tiffany. Hassan's discretions had come back to bite her, and Madison was devastated. She was still so naïve and blind that she had no clue who or what her father really was.

There, suddenly another knock, and SK's eyes shot over to the door. He nodded his head at his security.

"That must be the Door Dash people. Let that nigga in. I'm fucking starving."

Tone cracked the door just wide enough to be handed the food from the guy standing on the small porch.

"Nigga, I don't see no bags where the...." Meatcho aimed the gun up from the side of his right leg and put two bullets into Tone's face. He entered the front room first, followed by Hassan and Tiffany. SK dropped down behind Madison. So, you niggas had to come on some other shit. "Shoot at me, and you shoot your daughter, nigga," SK called from behind Madison, who was crying hysterically.

"I been itching to kill your bitch ass," Hassan stated. They couldn't believe that it was just SK in the building, alone with Camil. He should've had an army with him. He was making this shit too easy.

SK put his gun to Madison's head, and she flinched. That sight angered Hassan beyond words. "One wrong move, and she's dead. Tell that bitch and that nigga to get the fuck out. I won't care if you kill me, as long as I know I took this lil' bitch with me. Nah, fuck that. Put your guns down," he barked at Tiffany and Meatcho.

Tiffany and Meatcho both hesitated, and SK put a little

more bass in his voice. "Put the motherfucking guns down!" He looked at Hassan. "You too, nigga."

Tiffany knew she had to think quick. As she lowered her gun, she looked over at Camil. "Ma? You gonna let him do this?" Her voice quivered, and Tiffany could have received an Oscar for her performance.

Camil shot Tiffany daggers with her eyes as SK's head snapped in Camil's direction. "Ma? What the fuck she mean, ma? You told me this bitch was your goddaughter."

Camil's heart almost burst through her chest. "Baby, she's lying. She's desperate."

"How you think we knew where to come?" Tiffany added. "I'm her daughter, and Hassan is my father. She's been playing you this entire time. Camil can't be trusted. She's ready to let you kill her own child over a quick come up."

For the first time since knowing her, SK saw panic in Camil's eyes, and that let him know that she was guilty. He felt betrayed, and that enraged him. Just as Camil opened her mouth to beg, SK removed his gun from Madison's head and shot her in the chest. Hassan had to think quickly, and he used that opportunity to shoot SK. The bullet entered SK's neck, and his eyes immediately bulged out of his head in shock. Hassan had finally gotten his ass, and it felt good to Hassan. He walked over to SK and pumped more bullets into him. With each one, Madison's body jumped. Hassan knew she would never be the same, but they would have to deal with that later. When he was sure that SK was dead, Hassan untied his daughter and led her from the building. Madison was damn near inconsolable, but Hassan made her aware of how important it was that she do more walking and less crying. He just needed to get her away from there.

Tiffany and Meatcho went over to check on Camil. She was still alive, although bleeding profusely.

"Helppp meee," she managed to gasp while the blood filled her mouth. Tiffany looked down at her mother and was surprised that she felt nothing — no hurt, no desire to help, no joy, just nothing. Camil had done too many things, and the love and concern that should have been there just wasn't.

"What do you want to do? I know she's your mom, but leaving a witness is never a good thing."

"Nah, if she dies, she dies, but I'm not going to live with her blood on my hands. She's already emotionally dead to me. Leave her and let God decide."

In the car, Hassan breathed the hugest sigh of relief while he comforted both his daughters. The shit with SK was finally behind him.

———

Hassan braced himself for what he knew was to come. Chatima had been just as hysterical as Madison, and the both of them damn near needed tranquilizers to calm down. Chatima got herself together long enough to console Madison, and they were in her room in Madison's bed. Hassan had even assured her that Mack was stationed outside the house, along with three other security guards, and that nothing else would happen to her. Hassan apologized profusely and left Chatima to console Madison while he sat in his study, feeling like shit. The way his daughter cried, and the way Chatima screamed. Those sounds would be forever etched into his memory. Hassan wasn't afraid of much, but thinking that SK would shoot Madison in the head had damn near crippled him. Hassan would have sworn his heart stopped beating for a second.

He couldn't even fully celebrate the fact that SK and Camil were dead because of all that Madison had gone through. He had to credit Tiffany for saving the day. She had really come through. She was the one who saved Madison's life. When Chatima finally came into the study and her eyes met Hassan's, it was mistaking the fact that she was livid. "I don't want to traumatize my daughter any more than she's already been, but I'll put her in therapy. This is it, Hassan. I'm done. You've had numerous chances to walk away from this game, and you refuse. If you're not going to put your family first, then I'll do something about it. In the morning, I'm filing for divorce."

Chatima was sure when her adrenaline stopped pumping that she might regret her words to Hassan, but she was sick to death of worrying about him. Now, her daughter was put in harm's way. That was a dealbreaker for her. Not even the love she had for Hassan could make her ignore the heartbreak of what Madison had endured. Hassan glared at Chatima.

"You think you're going to take my daughter away from me?"

"You think you're going to stop me?" Chatima challenged. "I have tried my best to stay by your side. I fight your cases, I take care of your home, I raised your kids, but you won't do the one thing that will give this family some relief. I'm taking Madison out of harm's way. You can do what you want with Tiffany, but I won't continue subjecting Madison to this bullshit."

Hassan stood up and walked over to where Chatima stood. "I suggest you think long and hard about what you're saying to me."

"I have. I've been thinking about this for months, but you're too caught up in your own bullshit to recognize when I'm truly not happy. I didn't even get a thank you for getting your case with Camil dismissed. As I said, you continue being king of the streets of Charlotte, and I'll take my daughter, and we'll start a safe life somewhere your enemies won't be looking for us."

She left the room, and Hassan huffed like an angry bull. He wanted to tell her that she'd take his daughter over his dead body, but maybe she was right. Maybe she needed to move Madison somewhere safe for the time being. Even with SK out of the way, there was always some bullshit brewing in the streets, and who knew if some more drama was around the corner, waiting to rear its ugly head? Hassan wasn't going to fight Chatima on taking Madison as long as she knew that she'd never keep Madison from him. For the time being, maybe it was best.

———

Mack was waiting on her, and she had more business to handle before the night was over. Mack took her to Hassan, and she walked in the room and spotted him sitting on the couch with a glass of whiskey in his hand. Though his biggest headache had been wiped off the streets, Hassan still looked stressed, and she wasn't sure why because money was good. It was more than good. It was great.

She sat down on the couch and waited for Hassan to speak. He sipped his alcohol and looked over at her. "I want to thank you for all you're doing to hold my business down while I'm trying to get these crackers off my back. My business has turned into the family business, and you're doing a phenomenal job."

"Then why do you look so sad and stressed out?"

"Because Chatima took Madison and left. I can't really say I blame her, but that doesn't make it any easier."

"Damn," Tiffany mumbled. "I'm sorry to hear that. I'm

sure she's pretty shaken up from what happened. Just give them some time to process things."

Hassan chuckled. "Look at you, giving me advice. I'll certainly take that into consideration. SK might not be a threat anymore, but we had too many close calls when I was beefing with that idiot.

"You just home alone now? You really think Chatima isn't going to come back?"

Hassan shook his head and released a breath. "Who knows? She's been beefing with me for a minute. She's been upset because the Feds are on my ass, and they want me to snitch on Torres and accept a plea for five years. I'm not a snitch, and that's not even an option for me, so when they finally get my ass, I'll have to take whatever comes with it."

Tiffany wasn't sure how she felt about hearing that Hassan could go away for a long time. She had spent so much time hating him that now, she would be kind of sad if he got sent away. She still held scars from her childhood, but life had changed so drastically for her. She was getting money, and Tiffany finally had a parent. She had Jayden, but if Hassan went away, she felt that she'd be back to square one.

"That's not really good," she mumbled. Tiffany had been getting texts from Amar ever since seeing him in the trap house. She wasn't sure what she and Meatcho were developing, but she knew she wasn't interested in Amar anymore. A few of the texts and voicemails were full of sarcasm and envy about her status. He had already proven that he wasn't man enough to have a boss bitch as his woman. However, he seemed to be a good worker, and she didn't want to lose good earners; nor did she need to create anymore enemies. Texting him back, she agreed to meet him at an uptown bar.

CHAPTER 10

Tiffany walked into the bar and looked around for Amar. He had taken a seat near the rear entrance, close to the pool tables.

"Damn, you a hard woman to get up with," he joked as he stood up to give her a hug.

"I know. Sorry about that, but a woman who's not busy just might be a broke woman."

"So why didn't you tell me you're the plug? You said you came from money, but you damn sure didn't say anything about being Hassan's daughter."

"Why would I?" Tiffany asked with a frown. "I don't go around dropping Hassan's name for clout. Plus, who just goes around telling people they're the plug? That's not how I move."

"I get that, but I thought we were building, shorty. You keeping something like that from me is crazy. And who is that nigga you were with?" he questioned.

Tiffany chuckled. "Seriously? You standing here, grilling me about my business. We're not that deep, Amar. Just chill.

Just know that the day you saw me, I was at work. I was in hustle mode, and I kept personal and business completely separate. So, if you're not trying to cop some work what's the reason I'm here?"

Amar's gaze turned lustful. "You know why you're here. I want you even more now that I know you a boss ass bitch."

Tiffany scrunched up her face thinking, *was that supposed to be a compliment?* Too bad he fronted about being a boss ass nigga. Talking about his name was heavy in the streets, and he was merely slightly over a corner boy. He didn't even sell weight. And Tiffany even knew that workers who sold hand to hand could have heavy pockets, but he wasn't making the kind of money he portrayed himself to be making. It probably took him a week to earn what she made in a day. That was far from equal in her book, and she knew she wouldn't take him seriously as long as he remained under her.

She gave him a tight smile before speaking.

"Amar look, I really have a lot going on right now, so thanks for the drink, but let's talk about this another time."

"Damn, when you gon' stop treating me like a lame, and give me some real conversation? I'm saying. You're not the only one doing big things. Together, we can be running this shit."

He was talking about her money and her status a little too much for her liking. Ever since he found out who she was, that's all he'd been referencing. "I hear you, but I really have to go. We'll talk later." Tiffany knew as soon as she got in the car, she was blocking his number.

Amar didn't say anything else, and Tiffany left. By the time she got in the car, she was exhausted and ready to get home. Running Hassan's business was hard ass work. She earned every penny she made. Tiffany was so excited to reach her condo, she let herself get caught slipping. Seconds after she got out of her car, a masked gunman was up on her, pointing his gun in her side. Her eyes widened in shock. He must have followed her from the hotel, and she didn't even notice. She let being tired keep her off her game, and she was about to regret it.

Tiffany had a little money inside the condo. It wasn't everything she had, and she didn't have any drugs there. She wasn't too worried about what he might take. Unless, the man took her life. Jayden was also inside and very pregnant. Tiffany wanted to kick herself for bringing this type of drama to their home. Had she realized she was being followed, she would have led them into a trap.

"Walk," he instructed.

Tiffany's heart was beating a mile a minute. She prayed that Jayden would act fast and use one of the guns they had inside the condo. Even though they lived in a nice, upscale area, they knew to stay prepared at all times. Well, most times because Tiffany knew she had dropped the ball. She began to walk slowly.

"Pssssst."

The sudden, low noise from behind them made the gunman whirl around, and he removed the gun from Tiffany's side. Before he could adjust his eyes to the darkness, a blow to the face sent him staggering back. Tiffany was quick on her feet and leaned down and yanked the gun from him. A male came up and stood beside her with his Glock trained on her would-be robber, and she glanced over and saw that it was Meatcho.

"What are you doing out here?"

"I told your pops I would watch your back, and that's what I'm doing. When you said you had something to do, I went home and tried to relax but couldn't until I knew you were safely at home as well. I figured I would roll by to make sure and seen this nigga plotting."

At that moment, she had never been more grateful that Hassan decided she needed more muscle. Had Meatcho not taken it upon himself to check on her, there was no telling what would've happened at the moment.

"Thank you," she replied before returning her attention to the man getting up off the ground. She was tempted to fire a shot into his kneecap, but they were in the wrong neighborhood for that.

Meatcho hit him again and when he hit the ground again, Meatcho snatched the ski mask off his face and turned to Tiffany. "You know this nigga?"

Her eyes narrowed as she took in the light-skinned man's face. "No, I don't know this nigga. Who the fuck are you?" she barked.

The man remained quiet as Meatcho pulled out his phone. After a few seconds, he spoke. "I need a clean-up crew ASAP." The man's eyes widened, and Meatcho's grip tightened on the gun. "You can play tough all you want, pussy, but not answering our questions will only ensure that you die. The choice is yours. The clean-up crew is on the way, and they aren't far away."

The man sucked his teeth. "Amar sent me, man. He told me that a bitch was on the way to a hotel to meet him, and I could wait there and follow her to her crib. He told me she was a big fish, and I could probably get enough to be straight for a lil' while. I swear, I didn't even know who I was following."

Meatcho looked back over at her. "Who the fuck is Amar?"

"One of the bitch ass niggas in the trap this morning. I've

been dealing with him a little bit and up until today, he had no clue what I did or who I was."

Meatcho turned back to the guy, knowing he couldn't kill him out there. As soon as the gunshot sounded, police would be swarming the area. "Get the fuck up," he instructed.

The man stood up, and Meatcho's gun was damn near touching his nose. "Walk back towards your car."

The man did as Meatcho asked, but the entire time he walked, his brain tried to think of something to say to get him out of this mess. He should have never listened to Amar's ass. The lick sounded too damn easy, and now he could see that it had indeed been too good to be true. "I swear to God, if you just let me g—"

"Shut the fuck up," Meatcho growled. "Fuck we look like letting your bitch ass go? You wanted to be a gangsta, so now we're going to make sure you die like one."

The man's palms began to sweat, and he was panicking on the inside. The life he lived came with uncertainties, and death was always around the corner, but he wasn't ready to die tonight. Just as they reached his car, a black van pulled up, and the side door slid open. "Get in," Meatcho instructed.

The man peered inside the dark van and tried to make out how many people were inside. He knew once he got in that van, it was a wrap. He'd be taken somewhere to die a gruesome death. When he hesitated to climb inside the van, Meatcho hit him in the face with the butt of his gun. "I don't like repeating myself, nigga."

With a heavy heart, the man climbed inside of the van, knowing that he had gone on a suicide mission. Trying to rob Tiffany and get some fast cash was about to cost him his life, and he had no one to blame for it but himself. As soon as he climbed in the van, the door slid closed, and before it was closed all the way, a loud gunshot was heard. The van sped off into the darkness, and Meatcho looked over at Tiffany.

"You good?"

"Yes. I can't thank you enough for taking it upon yourself to keep following me. I have guns inside the crib, and my roommate is in there. She has a gun in her room. We may have been able to come out of the situation on top, but she's pregnant, and I'd rather not put her through that stress. So again, thank you."

"I'm just doing my job, ma. Hassan wanted me to look after you, and that's what I'm doing. You go on in and get yourself some rest. I'll be down here, keeping a lookout on everything."

"Meatcho, you don't have to do that. I'll be ok," she shook her head.

"I know you will, but I wouldn't be able to sleep anyway, just thinking about someone trying to come back and finish what that fuckboy started. I got our people out finding your boy now and after he dead, I'll go home."

Tiffany didn't want to argue, and she would feel safer knowing he was there. So, she turned and headed towards her condo. "What a fucking night," she mumbled. But before going in the door, she looked back as Meatcho was walking towards the parking deck.

"Hey, you want to come up? I don't think I'm going to sleep anytime soon."

"Do you want me to come up?"

"I wouldn't have asked if I didn't," she responded, biting her bottom lip.

He followed her lead up and into the apartment. The whole place was dark, except for the light under the microwave. Tiffany turned on the flat screen TV that was hanging on the wall, and they both took a seat on the large, white sectional sofa.

"Jayden must be sleeping. You know the pregnancy keeps her tired."

"Yeah, I've heard that. How much longer she got anyway?"

"Not long. It really can be any day now. Speaking of, I'm surprised a man like you don't have any kids. What you waiting on?"

"What you mean a man like me?" he laughed.

"I mean, you're smart, you're a hustler, and very pleasing to the eye. I imagine that you've had plenty of women who wanted to have your baby."

"Well, thank you for the compliment, and even if that's so, I wasn't trying to procreate with just anyone. You know the mother is the first teacher of the child, so, you need to make sure the mother is whatever you want your child to be . She can bless or ruin a life with her love, you feel me?"

"I definitely do, and I wish more men were so introspective. I've never known a mother's love, honestly."

"Have you ever known any type of love, Tiffany Scott?" The question caught her off guard. There was a time when she thought she had a real love with Nasir, but now, she wasn't so sure if it was love or infatuation. Hassan and her relationship was so new that their love as father and daughter was still developing.

"Honestly, I don't even know if I know what love is," she stated in a somber tone and dropped her head.

Meatcho stood up, walked over to her, and raised Tiffany's face up to meet his gaze.

"Love is patient, love is kind. It does not envy, it does not boast, it is not proud. It does not dishonor, it is not self-seeking, it is not easily angered, it keeps no record of wrongs. It always protects, always trusts, always hopes, always perseveres. Love never fails."

Tiffany was stunned by his words. He was speaking directly to her heart and soul. The love he was speaking about was all she desired and longed for.

Meatcho's lips met hers, and they shared a deep kiss. While they kissed, his hands roamed her body and made their way underneath her shirt. He broke the kiss long enough to pull her shirt over her head and remove her bra. He sucked on her neck while he massaged and groped her breasts. Tiffany closed her eyes when he pressed his hard body against hers, forcing her to lay back. Meatcho licked and kissed on her neck then down to her inner chest and stomach, all while simultaneously pulling down and off her tights. He spread her legs wide and moistened his mouth before moving down and taking his first taste of her honey pot. She was clean shaven, and the sensitive lips that kissed him back were starting to get sticky, making him desire to taste more of her. Placing his tongue deep inside her, he started moving it all around her pussy walls. Meatcho didn't want to miss a spot. Her moans only intensified his oral assault as he was now sucking gently on her clit while licking slowly on the outer lips. Tiffany had two handfuls of his hair, pulling him deeper inside her now semi-closed legs. He could tell that she was about to cum, and the screams of "please don't stop, baby" with the excess liquid now filling his mouth and face confirmed it. Her whole body went temporarily limp. But Meatcho wasn't done. He'd been wanting her ever since the first meeting at Hassan's house, and if this was his only chance, he was going to make the most of it. Turning her over on her stomach, just like before, he started at the back of her neck, then to the small of her back and finally spreading her ass cheeks, he placed his tongue into the center that was already wet from the rundown of the previous sessions. Tiffany didn't think it could get any more intense, but the action he'd just done sent chills down her spine. She had never had her ass eaten out, and the experience had her feeling like she was going in and out of consciousness. She grabbed onto the sheets, trying to steady herself because even though she was lying down, her balance was clearly off due to her head spinning. She was squeezing so tight, that her freshly manicured nails were piercing the skin of her palms. "Meatcho, please baby, I can't take no more." Those words made him extend his tongue as far as he could inside her ass. The second orgasm was about to come, and it was clearly going to be even more intense. He extended himself, knowing the next wave of pleasure that his tongue was about to give her. "Ohhh, Ohh, Oh, shitttttttt!" She screamed so loud, she knew Jayden had to hear her, but she didn't care because her whole body was burning with pleasure and was beginning to convulse.

"Baby, I want you to cum on my dick, ok?" Tiffany shook her head in agreement, and Meatcho guided all nine inches of his dick into her soaking wet pussy. Now he was the one making noises. Her walls were so tight and gripped his member like a newly fresh pair of gloves. The heat mixed with the friction had him increasing his speed and depth with every motion. He licked his middle finger before placing it inside her ass that his tongue had already laid the route for. Tiffany began rubbing on her clit, and the triple action of her finger, his dick and finger all playing together like a fine orchestra had her about to burst. "Cum for me, baby. Cum on this dick."

"Here I cum!" Tiffany screamed as her body released all the juices she had trapped inside. He could feel her inner walls starting to tighten, and experience told him he better hurry up and cum. So, he slowed his strokes, making sure that he savored every part of her insides. Brushing the hair off her face, he took in all her beauty and facial expressions. "You want to cum in this pussy, baby?" Her question was all he could stand. "Yesssssssssss, love." They both laid there in silence, saturated in one another's sweat and body fluids.

Meatcho was the first to get up and break the silence.

"You mind if I light one up?" he asked while heading over to his hoodie that was lying on the chair.

"No, it's cool. I might need to smoke one with you," Tiffany laughed.

He pulled out the already rolled blunt and lighter and fired it up before laying back down beside her. After taking a few toots, he passed it to her, and she did the same. The fresh weed hit her lungs with a brute force, making her cough the smoke back up. They both began to laugh.

"You got to be careful with that gas, ma, you heard me?"

"Yeah, I see that... Meatcho, can I ask you something?"

"Sure, anything."

"Did you make up that definition of love?"

Staring at her with a smile, he answered, "No baby, that's from the Bible, but I meant every word for you." Staring back at him with love in her eyes, all she could do was smile.

CHAPTER 11

Chatima looked up from her paperwork as she heard a light knock on her door. "Come in." She was surprised to see Tiffany stepping inside the office.

"Hey. Your receptionist wasn't at her desk. I hope it's okay that I came back."

"Yes. She's at lunch. Have a seat." Chatima waited for Tiffany to sit down. She noticed how different the girl looked. She looked older and more mature. Tiffany was dressed in a money green wrap dress and nude heels. "What brings you by?"

"My father told me what's going on with the Feds. He also let me know that you want him to take a deal, but he's not trying to snitch."

"Yes. Hassan's loyalty for the game runs deep. He knows that once they get him, they'll have enough of a case to give him double digit numbers, but he still refuses to give Torres up. So, there's nothing that can be done about that."

"As someone who's married to one of the biggest dope boys in the game, I'm sure you know that if he does decide to snitch on Torres, him getting a light sentence won't matter because he won't live long enough to get out."

"Look, as I told him, they're not even trying to have him testify, write any form of a statement, or any paperwork whatsoever. A simple heads up that Torres is on American soil, that's it. There's no way for it to trace back to him period."

"You really believe that? Torres is worth millions. He's probably worth billions. Nobody is that rich and powerful and in the game for that long without having plenty of people in their pocket, ranging from cops and judges to COs and politicians. It would be nothing for him to find out it was Hassan and have him touched. And if not Hassan, then someone in his family."

Chatima sighed. She didn't want to be rude, but she was trying to figure out why Tiffany was there. She had heard enough about why snitching was a no no. "Okay, Hassan isn't going to snitch. I've pretty much accepted that. You aren't telling me anything I don't know. I'll tell you that you and your father may know the streets, but this is my world, and I know the law and legal protocol."

"I know I'm new to the equation, and I don't want to feel like I'm overstepping my boundaries, but Hassan is walking around, looking like a lost puppy. It's like he lost his best friend. I know you feel like he chose the streets over you and the kids, but he really loves you."

Chatima smirked. "I think it's admirable that you want to defend your father, but you're right about one thing. You're new to the equation. This is years in the making. Hassan has chosen the streets over his family time and time again, and I'm just tired of asking him to choose. It's just that simple. Hassan had enough money to walk away from the game long ago. Now, his fate with the government is inevitable, and he still won't completely walk away. I'm done, Tiffany."

"What if I told you I figured out a way to possibly help Hassan?"

———

Hassan looked from Tiffany to Meatcho.

"Tiffany, the point of you having security is so you don't have to go out alone — that means, even if you're going to do something you don't think you need security for. Do you know how last night could've gone left?"

"I know, Hassan. I've learned my lesson. Even if I just need to go to the corner store to get gas, I won't go alone. Mack or Meatcho will be aware."

"Thank you for looking out for her," Hassan told Meatcho, and Tiffany felt a broad range of emotions. He thanked Meatcho like he was really grateful to him for saving her, and that made her feel emotional.

"It's no problem, man. I know how it is out here. Niggas see a female on top and automatically see an easy target. I didn't have shit else going on anyway. I can stay on the clock, 'round the clock if need be." Meatcho and Tiffany's eyes connected on the last statement of staying connected around the clock because they had been doing just that since that night.

"I definitely appreciate you."

Hassan and Tiffany wrapped their meeting up, and Hassan asked to speak to her privately, so Mack and Meatcho went outside. "You might be a little too old for lectures, but you really have to be careful of the company you're out here keeping."

"I know, Hassan. I met the nigga at the gas station, and he

didn't seem like a slouch. He appeared to have a little bit of paper, and he was just cool. I only hit him up when I felt like it. Every time he asked me what I did, I was vague. I told him I came from money, but I never gave any specifics. He tried to tell me that he was a heavy hitter in the streets, but I saw him at one of the traps when I went to pick up money. From there, I guess he just started plotting."

"In this game, you certainly have to have your head on right. There isn't room for distractions or weaknesses. If you have kids or anyone who's near and dear to you, they can easily become a target. But I don't advise you to stay alone for too long. That shit isn't good for you either."

"I'll keep that in mind. I promise, Pops. So, are we still on for the meeting with Torres this week?"

"Yep. Everything is still in motion. Someone will reach out to us soon on the meeting spot and time, and I'll let you know.

Tiffany left the house, and Hassan had to decide whether he wanted to spend another night alone in his big, empty house, or if he wanted to step out and hit up one of his old flings. In the last couple of years, He'd done a good job of keeping his dick in his pants. It had been a minute since he stepped out on Chatima, but he was still that nigga. There had come a time when Hassan had simply outgrown dealing with multiple women. Even though he was technically still married, Chatima made it clear that she was done, so why should he have to spend every night alone?

Hassan had made up his mind to change clothes and go out when he heard a loud ass bang. There were two sounds that came from different directions, one in the front of the house and one in the back of the house. Something stopped Hassan from getting his gun because he knew what it was. Instead, he grabbed his phone and checked his security app.

His whole body began to shake, and his stomach felt nauseous. All he could see was federal agents with guns drawn, running around the bottom floors of his home.

He heard footsteps running upstairs, and he remained standing still. He was going to wait in that very spot for them to come take him.

———

"Damn, so what do we do now? Does business just go on as usual?" Mack and everyone were now asking Tiffany. It was the next day, and word had gone throughout the city that Hassan had been locked up and with no chance of bail. The Feds never offered bail in high level drug cases; it was their way of trying to get people to break and snitch on any and everyone.

"Have you heard from your father?" Meatcho asked.

"No. I don't think they're letting him use the phone just yet. Chatima got in to talk to him as his lawyer, and she said they have him on lockdown. No phone calls and no visits until further notice."

"Damn," Meatcho mumbled. "That shit is tough."

"My Pops knew they were coming. It was just a matter of time," Tiffany offered. "For now, I think it's best we all lay low. There's no telling how much they already know, and there's no need to give them more to build a case on."

"Yo Ma, one thing about the Feds is, if they come get you, they already have their case. That's the difference between them and local law enforcement. The police arrest and then investigate, the Feds investigate and then arrest. So not for nothing, I still need to make a few moves to get myself situated, but I won't do it with y'all's involvement. A nigga got a goal I can't miss, because I know it's worth taking the chance for." Meatcho was looking at Tiffany, letting her know she was the goal he was talking about.

"Well, what if you could get the goal without taking any chances?"

"We both know that's not the case, and I know you need to do what you need to do for Hassan, and I respect and understand it. So don't you fix your mind to worry about me. I got this, and us, as soon as I'm straight."

"What will you do for product? You know I'm supposed to meet with Torres tomorrow morning."

"Baby, I just got done doing five years. You know how many connects I can get to." He laughed before grabbing her and pulling her close to him.

"Trust me, baby. You do whatever you need to do, and don't worry; I got your back, your front, and your sides. I've been around you long enough to know you'll make the right choices for us all."

––––––––

Tiffany could barely sleep that night and had been tossing and turning all through the early morning as well. She had received the call with the time and location to meet up with Torres. He was already aware about Hassan's incarceration but still wanted to meet to make sure she would be able to handle everything going forward. She had also been in constant contact with Chatima and had to admit, she was right about her knowing the law and the legal system. Tiffany admired the way she moved and handled the people so much, she was thinking about becoming a lawyer herself. If not that, something in the business world. The only other thing that had been on her mind was Meatcho. Even though he told her not to worry about him, she still was. His definition of love kept playing back in her mind, and she had actually screenshotted it to her phone.

Her thoughts were interrupted by Mack calling to let her know he would be there to pick her up in about an hour and a half. She got up and busied herself getting ready. Not really sure if she wanted to present herself in business attire or street wear, she decided to go business casual with some jeans, a sexy fitted blazer, and boots. Before leaving out, she made sure to check on Jayden.

"Good morning, I just wanted to make sure you were good and didn't need anything before I headed out."

"Morning, look at you, looking all good. I can't wait until I'm able to fit back into my jeans. But no, if I need anything, I'll just order Door Dash. Be safe."

Tiffany thought about those words and knew that what she was planning today could be everything but safe. She was making a decision that would either put everyone she loved into a new, bright future or could cost them their very lives. Picking up her trap phone, she took a picture of the coordinates that had been sent to her from the meet up and texted the photo to Chatima.

In the car, Mack was trying to have small talk, but her mind was too preoccupied with what she had going on to be able to carry on a conversation. Tiffany had second guessed herself enough to be sick, but she couldn't turn back now. She was going to have to let the cards fall where they may. Her stomach was in knots the entire ride, and she felt like she wanted to throw up.

"What the fuck?" she heard Mack exclaim as they neared their destination. They were about a mile from the meeting location, and Tiffany looked up to see seven black SUVs blocking the road. There was a helicopter flying above, and they weren't letting traffic through. "That looks like..." his voice trailed off, and a lump formed in Tiffany's throat.

"The Feds," she managed to choke out. She had given Torres up to the government, so that Hassan would get a lighter sentence. She knew he wouldn't approve, but if he truly loved her, he would forgive her, knowing she had done it out of her love for him.

CHAPTER 12

Tiffany walked into Jayden's hospital room with a smile on her face.

"Look at you," she smiled at Jayden, who was holding her tiny son, MJ, in her arms.

Jayden looked over at her friend and returned the smile. "I wasn't sure you were going to make it." Tiffany had been laying low ever since she gave Torres up to the Feds. She hadn't been back to the condo in three weeks.

"You know I wouldn't have missed this for the world."

"So, are you back to stay?"

"I'm not sure yet. Where I've been has actually been pretty peaceful. A bitch hasn't had to deal with the phone constantly going off, not running here, there, and everywhere, collecting money, and dropping off product. Shit, I don't even have to move with security or look over my shoulder. I've really been enjoying that."

"Yeah, I can imagine. Just thought it would be nice if you were here to help me with the baby."

"You know I'm going to do that regardless. Even if I just

pop in and out. I'm for sure going to make sure you're getting breaks and a good night's sleep a few times a week."

Jayden smiled happily that her friend wasn't going back on her promise to be there for them. It was scary having a baby without Mason being around to help, but with Tiffany, Jayden knew she could get through it.

———

Hassan looked across the visiting table at Chatima.

"Why didn't you bring Madison?"

"Madison is still going through a lot. You're going to have to give her some time, Hassan. She's coming around, but I'm not going to force it. Nasir will be here on his next break from school, and I talked to Tiffany this morning. She's just waiting to get put on the visitation list."

"Well, thank you for coming. I appreciate that."

"Hassan, I'm not a monster, and I don't hate you. I just got tired of feeling like I was coming last, and I decided to walk away, so my feelings wouldn't keep getting hurt. That doesn't mean that I want you here or that I will leave you to rot."

"I wasn't sure if Tiffany would reach out to me, or you, anytime soon." It didn't take Hassan long to figure out what she had done for him, and Chatima had pretty much confirmed it.

"Yeah, she knows how you feel, but I got to say, she really loves her Pops, as she calls you." Chatima and Hassan both laughed.

He still didn't agree with snitching, but now that he was doing his time, he had to admit that he wasn't mad at only having to do five years. It was shocking to him that she had even done that for him. Although they were still working on building a strong father-daughter relationship, the foundation had definitely been set. Her risking her life to give Torres to the Feds was some bold shit to do, but she had shot him, so if it was one thing she was, it was bold. Now that his fate had been sealed, he and his daughter would be tight as ever and not just because of the drug business.

Looking in his wife's eyes, Hassan decided to see where her head was at.

"So, are you just gonna go on with your life? Should I be expecting divorce papers in the mail?"

"Would you really care if you did?"

Hassan released a breath. He promised himself he wouldn't get stressed out while in prison. His motto was, it was what it was. If Chatima really did divorce him, he wouldn't cry about it. He just wanted to know what was up, so there wouldn't be any surprises.

"Chatima, I wo—"

"No, Hassan. I don't plan on filing for divorce."

A smile came across his face. That was all he needed to hear. She still felt some kind of way, and he had some ass to kiss but for the most part, he knew she wasn't going anywhere, and that made his day.

———

"This view is beautiful." Tiffany peered out at the water as she sat on the boat that she and Meatcho were having dinner on.

"Yeah, it is. It's really peaceful. I used to think that niggas who did shit like this with women were corny. Guess I turned into an old corny nigga, huh?"

"Or a grown one. Our mindsets change as we get older. Nothing wrong with that."

"Speaking of mindsets, I think it's time for you to start a

new one. Either build a business or sit back and let someone else take care of you."

Tiffany smirked. "Well, I don't know if being a kept woman would be something I could do. I was always told, 'if you give a man the power to feed you, you're also giving him the power to starve you.'"

"That could be true in some cases, but if you're dealing with a real man, I don't see that being an issue, especially if you're married and have his children."

Damn. Meatcho is talking about marriage and children, Tiffany thought to herself.

"Well, all I can say is maybe. Baby, you have to understand. It's not easy for me to put my trust in someone else. That, I'm sorry for."

Meatcho reached for the glass of champagne he ordered and refilled both their glasses.

"Ma, don't you ever say you're sorry because you could never be that, and you don't have to worry about anyone starving you ever again. I love you, Mami, you hear me? I will always be here for you, and that's why everything I make, I'll turn over to you because I trust you to feed me. And hopefully, in time, you'll feel the same way. So, let's toast to new beginnings."

Tiffany raised her glass and smiled. "To new beginnings."

The End

SNEAK PEAK OF TRAPSTAR

CHAPTER 1
LUCKY ME

A shiny 2012 White Range Rover Sport came to a smooth stop perfectly in the parking space. The vehicle was one of the trappings of success; a symbol of luxury. Behind the wheel sat a young gorgeous African American female named Brianna Campbell. Through her Dolce & Gabbana shades, she glanced down at the platinum Rolex watch on her wrist. It read one o'clock. She was right on time for her hair appointment.

As soon as she entered the hair salon, Brianna noticed that all eyes were on her. Still, she remained cool behind her dark tinted shades. It would take more than a few envious eyes to unnerve her. Although Hera by Him was an upscale hair salon, it wasn't free from the catty gossip that plagued every hood shop. As soon as Brianna strolled past, almost immediately the whispers and speculation began.

With of all the high priced designer accessories and clothes Brianna wore, the majority of the women assumed that she was some ball players' girlfriend or wife. The large six carat diamond ring did little to dispel those rumors. There was no denying that she was well kept. Her outfit and designer bag caused some insecure women to fall back into obscurity when they saw her. They knew all her accessories were real, while most of theirs were bootleg; cheap knock offs.

Usually all clients were required to wait in the sitting area until they were called by their stylist, but not Brianna. She strolled right pass the receptionist, heading straight to the back. The receptionist merely glanced at Brianna, but she didn't attempt to stop her. She recognized that Brianna was a regular. But besides that Brianna had a swagger about her that suggested that she wasn't to be messed with.

Her stylist seemed to light up when she saw Brianna coming towards her. It wasn't because she was happy to see her or that liked doing her hair either. Brianna paid well; it was as simple as that. The stylist knew that she wouldn't have to do another head that day. Once Brianna was done tipping her, she was going to be straight.

"Hey Bri." The stylist happily said. "I can set my watch to you girl, you always on time. I wish all my clients were like you."

Lauren was one of the few people Brianna knew she could never allow to get a peek into her life. She had witnessed first hand the way Lauren spoke about her other clients and their personal business. So no matter how friendly her stylist was to her, Brianna was always the same; nonchalant. She always gave her the cold shoulder, shutting down any attempts at them becoming too friendly. All the idle chit-chat that went on between stylist and client didn't exist when she took her seat in the stylist's chair. Brianna guarded her privacy like a celebrity. Brianna simply smiled in response to the comment.

After taking off her shades and placing them inside her

bag, she handed her personal items to her stylist, who put the bag under the counter.

In the mirror Lauren smiled as she examined different parts of Brianna's weave. She could feel Brianna watching her. She went from the front to the back inspecting her hair. When she reached the back she grimaced slightly. Thankfully Brianna didn't catch it.

A large scar on the back of Brianna's head had caused this reaction. Brianna's scar betrayed her pampered appearance. What in the world was a woman of Brianna's stature doing with such an ungodly scar was beyond Lauren. As a matter of fact it was the subject of debate whenever Brianna left the salon. To her credit the stylist never asked any questions, and Brianna never offered an explanation.

Lauren could tell she had been through some shit, but what she didn't know. She would have loved to find out.

Quickly pushing those thoughts out of her mind, she went to work. Meanwhile, Brianna casually looked around. While Lauren moved about in the booth Brianna took notice of her attire. She was dressed in a black t-shirt and black jeans. Brianna looked down to see what she had on her feet and instantly she got pissed.

"Fuckin' Jordan's!' She cursed to herself.

Those sneakers would be forever stoned in Brianna's memory. It didn't matter if they were worn by a male or female, she hated them. As she closed her eyes Brianna's mind began to trace back to the moment that she had not been able to erase. Suddenly her thoughts began to run wild.

———

The halogen headlights shone brightly from the four door European sedan, illuminating the entire garage. With a touch of a button, the garage door quickly closed. Calmly the two occupants of the car made their exit. Tre led the way inside the house. After placing his key into the lock, he entered the house and punched in his security code, deactivating the alarm. His girlfriend Brianna followed closely behind. The couple had just come home from a busy night on the town. Brianna loved going out, she like being in the spot light. But Tre was the total opposite. In Tre's line of work it was better to be talked about rather than seen.

The streets of Charlotte, NC were like a jungle, filled with both predators and prey. But by no means was Tre anybody's prey. On the contrary, he was just as dangerous as they came. But, to meet Tre for the first time one would never know. He had a very laid back disposition, and would rarely be seen in jeans or any of the latest urban wear. He had learned along time ago, that the quieter you were the easier it was to move.

Inside the luxurious confines of his townhouse, Tre breathed a sigh of relief. .

"Umm, that steak was good as shit!" he suddenly announced. "I'm full like a motherfucker."

He flopped down on the couch, kicked back and relaxed. Reaching for the television remote, he turned on the 63 inch plasma TV. Quickly he became captivated by the new Rick Ross video that was airing on BET. He was feeling extremely sluggish. The big meal he had eaten had begun to take effect.

Meanwhile, in the hallway Brianna began to get comfortable herself. She slipped off her high heel shoes, loosened the buttons on her blouse and made her way toward the living room.

"Hold on Big Poppa." Brianna said. "Don't go to sleep on me yet. I got something way better than that steak!"

To Tre that could only mean one thing, some good head. Like the old saying went, 'The way to a man's heart may have been through a man's stomach'. But for Tre it was threw his dick. He went fool over some good head. And nobody did it better, than Brianna.

Immediately, Brianna got down on her knees and went to work. Quickly she unzipped Tre's pants, reaching inside she gripped his dick, pulled it out and took it into her mouth. Brianna's mouth was warm and wet. She began licking and sucking on the head of his dick. She worked her way down until every inch was in her mouth. Moving faster and faster until she felt his dick grow harder and harder. Brianna used just the right amount of spit and suction. Tre drop his head back and sighed.

Again and again, he thrust his hips to meet her hungry mouth. With his eyes closed he enjoyed the moment.

"Damn baby Suck dat dick!" He cursed. "Do dat shit."

Tre's cursing didn't even bother Brianna. She was with whatever it took to get him off. She knew if she didn't, there were plenty other hoes, out in the streets, who would jump at the opportunity. She felt if he was going to stray, it wasn't going to be because of anything she did or didn't do.

"Cum in my mouth daddy!" Brianna demanded.

The commandment drove Tre crazy. He quickly obliged. A hot jolt of semen shot from his balls to the head of his dick, into Brianna's warm and waiting mouth. As soon as it came out, she gobbled it up and swallowed it down. When she had drained every last drop of his love juice, Brianna continued to suck on his dick. Unable to take any more, Tre tried to pry her lips off.

"Alright, God damn!" He exclaimed. "Brianna, that's enough."

From the floor, Brianna glanced up at her man. A sinister smile spread across her face. She knew it was a job well done.

Getting up off her knees, Brianna proudly stood above her man.

"Nigga, git up." She joked. "It wasn't all like that."

Tre lay on the couch in the fetal position, trying to regain the little bit of energy, he had just lost.

"Shiiitttttt!!!" Was all he managed to say.

Brianna insisted. "C'mon, Tre stop playin'. Git up and come wit me upstairs to the shower. Let's get ready for bed. "

"You go 'head." He told her. "I'll be up there in a minute."

"Promise."

"Promise!" He replied. "I'll be right up there as soon as I get myself together."

"Alright, hurry up!" She demanded. "We ain't finished yet. We got one more round to go."

Reluctantly, Brianna walked away to prepare for their next sexual romp to take place in the shower. She hurried along in anticipation of what was to come. She had just turned the corner, taking only a few steps out of the living room when suddenly two masked gunmen appeared.

With the barrel of a semi-automatic weapon pointed directly at her forehead, Brianna didn't utter a word. Instinctively, she backed up as the gunmen moved silently toward her. The TV successfully drowned out any noise they made.

Quickly, the two masked men pushed Brianna into the living room, brandishing their weapons on Tre. Caught completely off guard, Tre just stared in disbelief, wondering how in the hell had these two niggas gotten into his house without setting off the alarm system.

The larger one barked. "Nigga, make a move and I'm gonna let you feel this heat."

Immediately, the other man snatched up Brianna. Everything appeared to be moving in slow motion to her.

Brianna was violently shoved onto the couch. With a gun

pointed in her face, she couldn't do anything but stare. The gunman and his weapon were oblivious to her, for whatever reason her eyes were locked on the man's hand. All she could see was the word 'Smalls' in cursive writing tattooed on the bottom of his hand.

"Bitch, don't look at me!" The gunman growled. "Turn ya fuckin head'!"

Either Brianna moved too slowly or it wasn't fast enough. Whatever the case was the gunman, viciously slapped her. Brianna head recoiled violently from the blow. She fell back onto the couch with the taste of blood quickly filling her mouth.

"Ok, you know what it is. Just give us what we came for." The larger one demanded. "Now where the stash at?"

"Nigger ain't nuttin' here!" Tre snapped. "I don't eat where I shit."

Unfortunately, the gunmen didn't buy a word he was saying. Without warning the large man, began to pistol whipped Tre. He was thrown to the floor where he was kicked and beaten some more. Blood began to flow freely from a gash in his head.

"Nigga, you think this a muthafuckin' game huh?" He yelled. "Now, I'ma ask you one more time. Where is it at?"

By now Brianna was in a state of shock. She didn't understand why Tre didn't just give them what they wanted so they could leave. She thought it was just that simple.

"Look, I already told you niggas. Ain't nuttin' here." He muttered through a pair of swollen lips.

A third man entered the room. With a nod of his head, he motion to the one who had Brianna, to lift her up. His partner reacted by reaching down, grabbing a handful of Brianna's hair, and snatching her up off the couch. He placed one arm around her neck, the other hand clutched the gun that was pressed to her temple.

"Nigga, you better tell us what we wanna hear and fast." The other gunman spat. "The next muthafuckin' lie you tell, this bitch is dead! Now, where's the stash at?"

Though he was more than a little woozy, Tre was still defiant. He glared angrily at his two assailants. An evil thought ran through his mind, 'If I can get to one of my guns. I'm going to kill these motherfuckers.

Amongst all the commotion, the shouting, the threats and the violence, the videos were still playing on the television, a tomb like silence suddenly enveloped the room. The threat of death hung in the air.

For what seemed like an eternity no one said a word. Brianna eyes suddenly locked with Tre's. They seemed to sing a sad song. They pleaded with Tre to give up the goods. Still he stood his ground, refusing to say a thing.

Seeing this Brianna knew she would be forced to take matters into her own hands. She felt it was the only way to remedy the situation, since Tre wasn't talking.

"It's upstairs in the bedroom." She blurted out. "The money is upstairs in the bedroom in a suitcase."

'Damn!' Tre cursed to himself. He shot her an ice cold stare.

Tre would have rather her give up the location of the dope than the money. Money was too hard to come by. Now he had to take some more pen chances to recoup his cash. While if he was robbed of some drugs, he could go to his drug connection and get more on consignment.

The gunmen released his grip on Brianna, who stood there holding her throat. Trying to recover from the choke hold she had been in. Taking two steps away from her, suddenly the gunmen turned back around and viciously struck her with the butt of his gun. Caught off guard, Brianna went crashing face first to the floor. She was knocked unconscious by a blow to her temple.

The other two gunmen laughed heartily, signaling their approval.

"Damn, you knocked that bitch out cold." one commented. "Now go upstairs and get the money."

Doing as he was told, the second gunman fled the living room, and went to retrieve the money.

The larger gunman announced, "Nigga, ya girl smarter than you. You lucky she told us when she did. I thought we was gonna have to kill her ass, just for you to talk. Just for that we gonna let ya'll live."

Tre didn't believe a word the man had said. But he wasn't really focused on him anyway. It was the third man who didn't speak a word that concerned him the most. It was obvious he was the one running things.

Before Tre could give it any real thought or get himself together to mount an attack, he heard the other gunman come running down the stairs. It was then that he realized that he may have blown his only chance of survival.

"You got it?"

"Yeah, I got it! It was right where she said it was." He laughed.

Tre watched as the other gunman entered the room and gave the bag to third man. At that point he sensed that something was up, though no more words were exchanged between the men. It was as if he knew what was about to happen.

With two large caliber firearms trained on him, Tre watched as the men inched closer and closer, until they were within pointblank range. Something came over him that he hadn't felt in years, it was fear. Though he had personally sent countless individuals to the afterlife, now that it was his turn, suddenly he realized he didn't want to go. He wasn't ready to leave this earth, not at the ripe old age of twenty five years old. He had so much more living to do and things to see. He couldn't believe it was ending like this.

Tre wasn't a chump, but he knew he didn't want to die.

With the finality of the situation close at hand, Tre finally backed down off his defiant stance, his lumped shoulders now suggested he had gone into submission. A pitiful look appeared on his face, one that invited any act of divine intervention. Tre's look invited any act of mercy, so that his life and that of his girlfriend might be spared.

The gunmen shot him a cold look of indifference, one that seemed to suggest that they would not deviate from their plan. Their hard core looks condemn him and his girlfriend to their fate, which was death.

Suddenly without warning, Tre lunged for one of gunman's firearms. If he was going to die, he wasn't going down without a fight. Too bad he wasn't quite fast enough to execute his plans. Gunshots exploded through the room. Six bullets found their mark. When the smoke cleared Tre was slumped on the floor, dead.

"Now, finish the bitch! And let's get the fuck outta here!" The first gunman screamed.

Standing above Brianna, he had a chance to see her innocent beauty. Even though she was covered in blood, her face was captivating. He closed his eyes and fired two shots, one missed badly and other drew blood, but it only grazed her head.

Brianna lay motionless on the floor. The gunman thought he had successfully executed her.

Long after the gunmen were gone, Brianna continued to lie on the floor, playing dead. She wanted to be sure no one was going to double back, to finish the job. As she looked around, she saw Tre's lifeless body lying in a pool of blood. For a long time she lay there thinking about Tre. It was heart-breaking to see him like that. Though he was certainly no angel Tre didn't deserve to go out like that.

––––––––

That night at the hospital, a weeping Brianna sat for hours answering every question that the police threw at her.

"Ma'am, could you tell us why someone would want to hurt you and your fiancé?" The older white cop asked.

"You said robbery earlier, but it didn't seem like they took anything of value." The other cop spoke.

Brianna knew she couldn't tell them exactly what happen, there were still drugs at the house. And she didn't know how much. She cleverly sprinkled lies in with the truth. She knew she needed to get home and get the dope out the house. Or she would not only be losing Tre, but possibly her freedom. The FEDS didn't care who did the time as long as someone did it.

When the police left, Brianna checked herself out the hospital. She couldn't bring herself to stay in the house that night. So she checked herself into a hotel. While she lay on the bed, she looked up at the ceiling. She wished she had a family to lean on, but she knew hers was not an option. Her family life had never been what a little girl deserved. Espe-cially one who had both parents. This was now her second time, being alone, and having no one to turn too. As she fell asleep she reflected on her childhood.

CHAPTER 2
HARD KNOCK LIFE

Brianna Campbell always has been a dreamer. She loved fairytales with happy endings. Ever since she was a child she loved to pretend. Brianna was a latchkey child, raised on unhealthy amount of television and movies. She idolized black actors and actresses, to the point that she could quote and re-enact some of the most famous parts, line for line. Her room was like a sanctuary.

Life in the Campbell household wasn't the same for Brianna as it was for her two other younger siblings, Jonathan and Charrise. Almost from day one, she sensed that there was preferential treatment shown to her younger sister and brother. It wasn't until she was around nine years old that she found out the reason why. At Brianna's ninth birthday party things finally came to a head. And the truth was revealed.

———

"How old are you now? How old are you now..." The partygoers chanted.

In the darkened kitchen, the nine candles on the store bought chocolate birthday cake, illuminated the room. Brianna hovered dangerously close to the cake, staring into the candles as if she were hypnotized. She enjoyed being the birthday girl, the center of attention. Sadly, she knew that her moment in the spotlight would fade quickly. Still she lived in the moment. Like any good actress, Brianna played her part well. Outwardly, she grinned ear to ear at her adoring guests. Inwardly, she hurt badly.

As she scanned the room, looking at each familiar face, one was noticeably absent, her Dad's. For some strange reason, he never participated in anything dealing with her. By now, it was routine, still it didn't hurt any less. She always noticed that he constantly shied away from her. Often Brianna wondered what she had done to deserve this.

"Brianna blow out the candles baby and make a wish!" Her mother urged her.

"Ok."

Inhaling deeply, Brianna summoned all the air her tiny lungs could hold and blew out the candles. Momentarily the kitchen went pitch black; the partygoers began to cheer loudly. When the lights came back on tears could be seen running down Brianna's rosy cheeks. Despite how it appeared, these weren't tears of joy.

"Oh, look at her she's so happy she's crying." One parent suggested.

But Lorraine Campbell knew otherwise. If there was one thing she knew, it was her children. She knew their temperaments and tendencies. And this was completely out of character for Brianna. She wasn't emotional at all. Lorraine sensed that something was very wrong.

Gently her mother took Brianna by the hand, and whisked

her away from her guests. She led her straight to the bathroom.

"What's wrong with you?" She asked. "What are you crying for?"

Though she tried her best to keep her composure, Brianna couldn't. Her tears continued to flow freely, now her body was racked by long hard sobs. Young Brianna merely stood in front of her mother unsure of what to say or do.

Her mother replied, "Don't just stand there looking all sorry. Say something! How else will I know what's the matter with you?"

After shedding a few more tears, finally Brianna mustered up the courage to tell her mother exactly what was bothering her.

"Where my Daddy?" She began. "How come he never comes to my birthday parties, huh? He always here for Jonathan's and Charrise's."

Her question caught Lorraine off guard. She hadn't expected this at all. But in the back of her mind she knew this day would come.

It was Lorraine's turn to be dumbfounded. She didn't know where to begin. But she knew that she had some explaining to do and fast.

"Brianna," She began. "The man you know as your father is not your father. He's your sister's father and your brother's father. But he's not your father."

Brianna exclaimed, "Huh? I don't believe you. You're a liar mommy!"

Brianna began to have a temper tantrum, she flailed her arms wildly at her mother. Dozens of light blows rained down on her mother's mid-section.

Unable to control her daughter's violent outburst, Lorraine

reached down and viciously slapped Brianna across her face. This seemed to bring her back to reality. Pain exploded across her cheek. She stopped her antics and clutched the side of her face.

Through clenched teeth her mother spoke, "Listen Miss and listen good. Herman is not your father. He is nothing to you. You and him have no blood relations. And that's that!"

Though Brianna couldn't comprehend everything her mother had said. But she understood enough. She got the message loud and clear. From that moment on Brianna was forced to grow up fast. She didn't like her mother's explanation but she had to accept it. For now it would be the only one she would get. It would be years before she knew the whole story.

Her mother and her stepfather, Herman, were high school sweethearts. When Herman went off to the army, following graduation, Lorraine had gotten weak and had a one night stand. Brianna was the product of that affair. But since Herman came home on leave around the same time she had gotten pregnant, and they too had intercourse, she chose to blame Herman for the paternity of the child.

The other guy was a local thug, who had nothing going for himself, other than being handsome. On the other hand, Herman had plans and goals that he was working towards. He was merely using the military as a stepping stone.

Some years later, unable to deal with her guilty conscious any more, Lorraine admitted her mistake to her husband. She received a severe beating as a reward for her honesty. Still Herman couldn't bring himself to leave his family. Against his better judgment, he stayed. Herman too was the product of a broken home. To his credit, he wouldn't let one act of infidelity break up his happy home.

Even though Herman had forgiven Lorraine, he could never forget. Everyday he was reminded of her infidelity when he looked at Brianna. He grew to despise her. As the years went on, he became abusive towards her. Not physically but mentally. Sometimes that was just as bad. His harsh words stung Brianna.

'You ain't cute. I don't know what you stay in the mirror for all day?' he commented. 'You ain't shit! And you ain't never gonna be shit! Your sorry ass daddy wasn't shit! Look he don't even care about you!'

Brianna was an A/B student, passing her classes with flying colors. One marking period she hadn't done so well. She received two C's. And her stepfather seized the opportunity to criticize and degrade her.

He spat, "Look at this shit here! You're so stupid. How you gonna fail gym?"

Her stepfather had degraded her time and time again, right in front of her mother. When she looked to her mother for support, she got none. Not once did her mother come to her aid and defend her. She did what she always did; Lorraine pretended not to hear it. Little by little, this caused Brianna to have animosity and resentment towards her mother.

Since Herman had money, he got away with murder around the house. Lorraine tolerated his cruelty towards her daughter because he was a good provider. A local businessman, Herman owned a string of soul food restaurants throughout Charlotte. She was just as much a dependent as her children were on her husband. She dared not voice her opinion in any way shape or form. She did her best to avoid the wrath of Herman. Lorraine knew when Herman got mad he got even financially by withholding funds.

Even though her younger sister and brother weren't nearly as bright as her, they always seemed to get the benefit of the doubt. When they failed a class, they failed because the teacher didn't like them. When she failed it was because she was just too dumb.

Over the course of time, her stepfather succeeded in slowly stripping her of her self-esteem. Brianna's grades began to suffer. She became a prisoner in her own home. She chose only to leave her room for one of three things, to go to school, use the bathroom and to eat. She avoided her stepfather as if he had an infectious disease.

Lorraine felt her daughter's pain, but truthfully she was powerless to stop the abuse. With her husband's blessing she decided to seek out Brianna's father. Secretly Herman had hoped that the girl's father would take her to live with him.

One day, Lorraine walked into her daughter's room and surprised Brianna. She told her to hurry up and get dressed, that her father was coming over to meet her. Instantly Brianna's face lit up, she felt reinvigorated as if a burden had been lifted off her.

Brianna got dressed in her best clothes, she raced downstairs and sat on the front porch eagerly awaiting her dad. Each passing car carried Brianna's hopes for a better life. And with each passing car, she was devastated more and more. Hours went by, with no sign of her father. Still Brianna didn't move from that spot, she never gave of hope. She sat there until the sun began to set. Finally, her mother had seen enough, she summoned Brianna inside the house. Lorraine was just as disappointed and heartbroken as she.

"C'mon in the house, Bri. That nigga ain't coming!" She cursed. "Don't worry about it baby. He missed out on a good thing not meeting you. It's gonna be alright! I promise, it's gonna be alright!"

Her mother's reassuring words did nothing for her. If anything they contributed to her ill feelings. Silently she cursed the day she was born. All she ever wanted was a mother and a father. Was that too much to ask for?

Tears began to well up in Brianna eyes. Suddenly she took off like a rocket, racing up the stairs. When she reached the second floor, she spotted her stepfather exiting the bathroom. He had a shit eating grin pasted to his face as their eyes met.

Brianna continued to run, racing past him to her room. She slammed the door and locked it. Throwing herself on the bed, she cried herself to sleep.

All throughout her formative years, Brianna had to endure this treatment. She became a stranger in her own house to everyone but her younger sister Charrise. The two had to keep their friendship a secret. She was the only person in her household that showed her genuine kindness. Maybe she wasn't going to be shit after all.

———

The Westside of Charlotte had long been a breeding ground for top flight hustlers and ruthless killers. That was where Treshaun Ellis, aka Tre, hailed from; LaSalle Street, the Betty's Ford section to be specific.

Almost from the time he was born, his life revolved around the streets. Both of Tre's parents were hustlers. His father Wally was a low level drug dealer. And his mother Marva was a booster, who stole clothes, for the entire neighborhood to buy. At one point or another, one or both of Tre's parents were in prison serving time for their parts in some botched crime. Subsequently, young Tre was raised by his maternal grandmother, on and off.

A day young Tre would never forget was the day his parents were killed. Fresh out of prison, Marva was looking extremely beautiful; Wally concocted a scheme to make money. He sent her out into the nightclubs of Charlotte, with form fitting clothes, in search of hustlers. Marva would then bed the hustlers, sexing them on a regular basis. As she did so, she gathered information on them. Like where they lived, what kind of guns they had or how much money was in the house. Their plan met success the first few times. Wally and his friend successfully robbed a few weak hustlers. With each conquest, the couple grew greedy for more.

Word had quickly spread on the street about the duo. They had gone to the well one too many times. After robbing one big time hustler, a hit was placed on them. Shortly after the order was given, Wally and Marva were found dead in the trunk of a car. They were both shot execution style in the back of the head. There were no witnesses to the crime and police never captured the triggerman.

Death seemed to further complicate Tre's already nomadic life, leaving a void in it. The murder of his parent's left him feeling more vulnerable and more broken than ever. He grew up thinking life wasn't fair.

From that point on, young Tre knew that life had no happy endings in store for him. He figured that his life could be only what he made of it. With both sources of income gone, Tre slowly began to gravitate towards the street. His neighborhood was filled with negativity and eventually he felt obliged to engage in it.

Originally, Tre got into the game to provide for, not only himself, but his grandmother too. He saw her struggling for the basic necessities, food, clothing and shelter. He didn't want to become another added burden upon her.

Around that time, Tre began to have a strange fascination with streets. With negativity all around him, he began to look up to the local drug dealers. They had money, the finer things in life, jewelry, pretty women and expensive rides that they flaunted on a regular basis. There was one drug dealer in particular that Tre idolized, named Petey. Tre worshipped the ground Petey walked on. After all, Petey was a ghetto superstar.

Petey believed that life came down to dollars and cents; either you had money or you didn't. It was as simple as that. He was prepared to hustle to get it.

Only five years older than Tre, Petey carried himself like a much older hustler. Just like Tre, he came from a family of hustlers; his daddy ran a pool-hall speakeasy and his older brother was a dope boy. Petey's entire family was involved in the game, in one way or another. It was almost expected that he would follow suit. And when he did no one even raised an eyebrow.

Out of all the kids in the neighborhood, Petey took a liking to Tre. This was because Tre would do anything he asked of him. Petey was no fool, he knew a soldier when he saw one. For the disenfranchised black youths like Tre, he was a godsend.

Petey was a smooth dude, he was a lover and fighter, a gangster and a gentleman all rolled up into one. He was everything Tre wanted to be. But most of all he was a character who had game for days. There was always a reason behind everything he did.

"Nigga, you got some money in ya pockets?" He would always ask.

"No." Tre replied. "I ain't got nothin'."

"Here's a lil sumthin' sumthin'!"

From a thick wad of bills, Petey peeled off a crisp twenty dollar bill and hand it to Tre. His eyes lit up, like it was Christmas. There had never been a time in his life that anyone just given him something without expecting something in return. That random act kindness went a long way with Tre.

It instilled a sense of loyalty in him for Petey. From that day forward, no one could ever say anything bad about Petey; not around him. Talking bad about Petey was like talking bad about his late mother.

Petey became like a big brother or mentor of sorts. Soon Tre became his sidekick, his 'little partner' as Petey referred to him as. Before Tre knew it he was running errands for him. Half of the time he didn't know the danger he was in. Tre became a drug courier, helping to distribute Petey's poison all over town.

For his efforts Tre received little or no money. Petey gave him just enough so that Tre would always need him. When it came to the drug game Petey passed along whatever wisdom he could impart and Tre soaked it all up like a sponge.

Like so many other young black males in the neighborhood, Tre viewed the drug game as his ticket out of the ghetto. He immersed himself in the murky, shark infested waters. Sink or swim, he was all in.

"Look nigga, you gotta always make sure you got a least three broads on ya team. The first broad she ain't a hood chick, should either work or go to school getting' an education. She wants somethin' out of life. That's your future wife. The second broad is a soldier; she holds the money and the work at her crib. She gotta be trustworthy. That's your vice president; if somethin should happen to you then she can take over. And the third broad she just a hood rat, somebody from the neighborhood you can keep the product at her house if needed. Even turn her house into a dope house if necessary." Petey explained.

These were rules to the game that Tre would always remember. He knew that they were tried and true because he watched Petey implement them everyday. As time went on

Tre became more valuable to Petey. He carefully played his position while patiently waiting his turn.

Sadly just like everyone else Tre ever loved, Petey died tragically, but not by an assassin's bullet. The word on the street was that Petey was poisoned. Although there was no medical evidence to substantiate such a claim, Tre had his suspicions. Women were Petey's Achilles heel; he was never good with them. So Tre trying to find the killer to avenge him was like finding a needle in a haystack. Petey had too many.

Tre had been the one to find Petey and rush him to the hospital. He was there at the hospital, along with a few members of Petey's family, when in the predawn stillness, he took his last labored breath.

The mournful sounds of his mother's cries, along with the steady bleeps and hisses of the life support machines, could be heard throughout the room. It shattered the eerie silence of death. Unable to bear it, Tre exited the room to mourn his mentor's passing.

Petey's death would prove to be bittersweet to Tre. He was thrust into the role of the man, in the hood. His only wish was that Petey was still alive to see it.

As a result of Petey's passing a bloody drug war ensued. The death toll seemed to mount daily. Dealers were scrambling to takeover the turf that once belonged to him. Quickly Tre had organized a team that took on all comers. When the smoke cleared Tre had emerged victorious. But he would forever be a marked man.

Just like Petey had controlled the neighborhood drug traffic for years, so did Tre. He ruled the neighborhood drug game with an iron fist. His reign of terror enabled him to hold it down for several years by instilling the fear of God in his rivals. Murder was his favorite weapon of intimidation. Whenever there was a problem, he made examples.

———

Seeking to getaway from the house, on the way home from school Brianna made a short diversion to Eastland Mall. It was a trip that would forever change her life.

For hours, Brianna window shopped at every store from Foot Locker, the Downtown locker room to Marshall's. She dreamed of owning all the name brands that she saw in those stores. Her stepfather treated her like a step-child in every sense of the word. When it came time to buy her school clothes, he made sure she got little or no money. Most times, Brianna's mother would have to take money from the other children's shopping allowance.

Standing outside of one store, Brianna starred at the mannequin that was modeling a cute pink Rocawear tennis skirt with a matching shirt. Unbeknownst to her, a pair of guys had slid up behind and began admiring her body. Even though she was shabbily dressed there was no denying her body or her beauty.

The moment Tre laid eyes on her, it was clear that he was attracted to her. He was smart enough to look pass her less than up to par apparel. He saw what her step father would never see; potential. He was awestruck by her beauty. Tre knew he had to have her.

"You'd look good in that." He said with a playful smirk. "Girl I can see you now."

Brianna simply smiled; she didn't know what else to do. Even at seventeen, she wasn't used to boys approaching her.

"You want that?" He asked. "Say the word and it's yours."

Brianna shot the handsome stranger a perplexed look that seemed to say, 'You can't be serious.' Still she felt she had nothing to lose and everything to gain.

"Well, if you wanna buy it for me, I'll take it." She said meekly.

He replied, "C'mon beautiful let's go get it."

This chance meeting turned into a makeshift shopping spree. Brianna entered the store with intentions on only getting one outfit. Instead she came out with an entire wardrobe.

After they finish shopping Tre took her out to eat. It was there that they learned more about each other. Instantly Tre knew that this was one of the chicks that he needed in his life. He felt that Brianna was wifey material, just like that his mentor Petey had described. She was green to the streets so he knew that he could easy manipulate and mold her. Her good looks were just icing on the cake.

On that day, fate had finally smiled on Brianna. It had brought someone in her life that could not only care for her but support her emotionally. She didn't have that type of support at home. Tre would become her mother and her father. Someone she could turn to in times of need.

———

After a year of courtship, when Brianna graduated from high school, she moved in with Tre. When she left home, her mother didn't so much as protest her move. Things had gone from bad to worse. Her husband and her daughter couldn't stand the sight of each other. Besides, she had two other children to worry about. Silently she wished her daughter well.

CHAPTER 3
WHERE'S THE LOVE?

Death never comes at a good time. For Brianna its timing couldn't have been worse. Her boyfriend had left so many loose ends behind it was ridiculous. Most people don't plan for their death, especially not drug dealers. When one lives on the outside of the law, they tend to live in the moment, so there are no wills. There is no paper trail to trace money owed out to them or their hidden assets.

Since Tre was in the upper echelon of drug dealing, this only compounded the problem. After his passing, everyone immediately assumed that Brianna was sitting on some dough, especially Tre's relatives. Their inquires about his finances and assets lead her to believe that they were more interested in that than finding the people who were responsible for his death.

Fortunately, Brianna was able to collect enough money off the streets to give Tre a proper burial. She managed to have a little left over for the bare necessities. After that she was hard pressed to crap up another dime.

Some dealers who had owed Tre large amounts of money for drug packages given to them on consignment, balked at paying giving Brianna the runaround, claiming they had already paid or just they didn't answer their phones. However bad they felt about his death, they weren't about to take a step backwards. This was the ultimate come up, one that had put many of them on their feet. They were not about to blow that once in a lifetime opportunity by showing some sense of moral responsibility. Any thoughts that they had of doing a good deed, like handing over the money, were an afterthought.

Brianna was left to bear the brunt of this burden. Right after the funeral everyone started showing their true colors. It was clear to her that all the love she had enjoyed while Tre was alive was long gone. Everybody was in flip mode.

For days after the funeral, Brianna did a combination of two things. She moped and mourned around the house that she had once shared with her boyfriend, unsure of exactly what was in store for her in the future.

One thing about being alone in the house that Brianna enjoyed was that it was alive with memories of Tre. All around the house there were various photos of him, riding in his big boy truck, the Infiniti QX56 SUV with '24 inch chrome rims. Some photos showed the couple spending a night out on the town. Others showed him posing for pictures at the club with his boys.

Tons of images seemed to flash through her head, as she relived the lasting memories that they shared. One image that would be forever be etched in her memory banks was Tre lying on the floor next to her, dead.

According to the Coroner's report, the official cause of Tre's death was a gunshot wound to the back of the head. But

Brianna knew the real cause of death. His tragic death had been caused by his life in the streets.

She stared at the pictures for hours on end. They became therapeutic to her, a way for Brianna to cope with Tre's death. They reminded her of a time in the not so distant past, when it was all good. It made her realize how quickly sugar can turn to shit. One could work a lifetime to acquire material things, or a good relationship for that matter, and lose it in the blink of an eye.

Still it was her present situation that disturbed her, life without her man. She wondered what she was going to do without him.

There was no doubt that Tre was her nigga; to know him was to love him.

———

"Ding, Dong! Ding Dong!" The bell sounded.

Even in her sleep, Brianna had heard the bell. She thought she was dreaming though. So she continued in her slumber.

"Ding Dong! Ding Dong!"

The sound of the doorbell shattered the silence of the house. Brianna knew that it wasn't a dream. Someone was at her front door. She wondered who it was. She hoped it wasn't the police coming to interrogate her again.

Slowly Brianna rose from her bed, gathering her bearings. She slipped on a large fluffy white bathrobe and a pair of Nike slippers, which had formally belonged to Tre, and headed downstairs to answer the door.

Ding Dong! Ding Dong! Ding Dong! The doorbell began to go berserk.

Just a few feet away from the door, Brianna's curiosity

was suddenly over taken by anger. She wanted to know who the hell was ringing her doorbell like that.

"Who is it?" She barked.

There was no answer.

"Who is it?" She screamed again.

Brianna was on fire, somebody was at her front door playing games and she was not in the mood for it. All things considered.

Without thinking Brianna unbolted a series of locks and snatched the door open. To her surprise, Tre's aunt Angie and his cousin, her daughter Yvette stood in front of her. She was frozen at the sight of them.

Suddenly, Brianna's mood went from bad to worse. She knew that their appearance at her front door wasn't a good-will mission. And they weren't there to offer their condolences.

"Good morning?" Angie greeted her. "You mind if we come in?"

Not waiting for a reply the two women barged right past Brianna.

"Come on in!" Brianna said sarcastically.

As soon as they entered the house, the two women began scanning the premises for valuables. As if it was an auction. No matter how hard they tried their eyes couldn't hide their intentions. They were like vultures on a dead carcass; they were there to pick the body clean.

To her credit Brianna already knew what it was. She had felt their vibe a few days ago at the funeral and everyday thereafter. She had expected them to show up. The only question was what had taken them so long?

"Damn! Ya'll was ballin' fa real." Yvette exclaimed, as she looked around the state of the art living room.

Brianna just stared at her blankly. She wasn't even going to dignify her with a response.

Brianna hadn't liked Yvette from day one. She had it out for her, Yvette tried and kept trying to put her girlfriends onto Tre. Over the years, they had had dozens of verbal altercations over the matter. Each side issued threats but never once did they come to fisticuffs, because Tre wouldn't allow it. Now that the peacemaker was gone, it was open season on Brianna.

Angie suddenly announced, "Look, Bri I'm goin' to cut right to the chase. The reason we're here is to pick up some things that my nephew Tre had promised me. He always told me, if anything ever happened to him that I could come over and take anything I wanted..."

Yvette replied, "Funny, he told me the same thing."

Brianna shot her a look that seemed to say, 'You-can't-be serious.'

She knew that Angie was lying through her teeth. Tre wasn't real close to anyone in his family, except his grandmother. He'd felt like his family was nothing but a bunch of leeches. No matter how much he gave them, they were never satisfied. They always had their hand out. In spite of that, he took care of them out of a sense of loyalty.

"Yeah, anyway!" Angie countered. "Since I was his favorite Auntie and everything, he said he would feel better if I had it."

"Oh yeah?" Brianna shot back with her arms folded across her breasts.

"Yeah!" Angie said with emphasis.

In the background, Brianna could see Yvette posturing with her hands on her hips. This provided Brianna only a hint of their collective foul mood. The sinister smirk that had spread across her lips seemed to tell it all.

The tension in the house was thick. At any minute violence could explode. Both parties took defiant stances, glaring at one another. Quickly Brianna weighted her odds, she ruled out striking Tre's aunt. She knew that if she fought one, then she would have to fight them both. And that they would most defiantly jump her. With these two ghetto dwellers there was no telling just how far they would go.

"Look, this shit don't mean nuttin' to me. Take whatever you want." She told them. "I'm in love with Tre! Not his possessions."

"Whatever, Bitch!" Yvette snapped, trying to instigate a fight.

Brianna shook her head in disgust; she took pity on these two savages. One of Tre's famous sayings suddenly came to mind. 'Don't become too attached to this shit. The drug game and life is so funny. What takes you years to get, can take you less than twenty minutes to lose.'

Brianna was in an awkward situation, on one hand she felt that she was entitled to everything. On the other, she felt indebted to Tre's family, but not these two, after all blood was thicker than water. She had only known him a few short years and they a lifetime.

A concession had to be made. Out of respect for Tre, Brianna decided not to make a big deal of it. The material items in the house could be gotten again, more expensive items at that. Still that notion didn't stop her ill feelings toward them. In her book they were just grimy. There was no other way to explain their actions.

Tre must be rolling over in his grave. She mused. Spurred by disappointment, Brianna went upstairs to her bedroom and locked the door. In silence she listened as the duo pillaged the house.

"Ohh, Mommy lemme have the microwave, you already got the blender." Yvette said.

Brianna listened intently as the two scavengers fought over who would get what. It was sad to see just how petty, two human beings could be. It was also disheartening to see just how death bought out the worst in people.

Upstairs in her bedroom Brianna paced the spacious room, back and forth like caged animal. She had to do something to rid herself of this nervous energy. She had to do something to keep herself from going back downstairs and jumping on somebody.

Impatiently she bided her time, in her bedroom, for what seemed like an eternity. Suddenly just as quickly as the commotion started, it came to an end. The quietness that engulfed the house was a sign to Brianna that the intruders were gone.

Quickly she went into her closet and opened a storage bin that was hidden way in the back. She pulled out a pair of old blue jeans and a bleached stained red t-shirt. In a hurried fashion, she put the clothes on. Then Brianna raced down stairs, through the house, into the backyard, it was time to dig up Tre's drug stash.

Tre wasn't too big on telling Brianna everything. Or any woman for that matter, he thought women were weak. If enough pressure was applied by law enforcement authorities, they would break. Tre didn't want to tempt fate. He always said 'what you don't know you can't tell.'

Fortunately over the years, he had grown comfortable with Brianna. He began to let her in on some of his secrets. Just in case anything ever happened to him. As it turned out this would be the most crucial one of all.

As soon as Brianna entered the backyard, she stood still. A puzzled look masked her face, as if she was trying to recall something. Scanning the yard she looked for a tool to assist her task. Leaning against the house she spotted a garden hoe. After taking the tool into her hands, she went about her business.

Retracing her steps, Brianna began her expedition at the back door. Slowly she took eight paces straight ahead, then made a sharp right and took four more paces. Where she stood, supposedly, x marked the spot. The dope was literally beneath her feet, buried in a shallow hole in the soft earth.

Burying this stash of dope was totally Tre's idea. He used to do this as a youth when he sold drugs out of a dope house. To avoid being robbed or caught by the police with large packages of drugs, he buried them in a nearby wooded area, taking only what he thought he could sell. This was a brilliant stroke of genius, not once did Tre loss a single gram, adhering to this system.

Brianna was sure that it was the right spot. With all her might, she brought the hoe down tearing away at the patches of grass. Powerful strokes from the hoe began to tear huge chunks of earth and grass. Soon Brianna began to break a sweat. She kicked away all the debris and fell to her knees. With her bare hands she began digging away like a dog. At a feverish pace, she attacked the earth as if it were a bitter enemy.

Brianna was glad it was still early, her neighbors most likely were at work and so no prying eyes would witness the extraction of drugs from the earth.

"God Damn!" She cursed. "Where the fuck is it?"

Just as Brianna was about to lose hope, her hands unearth some plastic. She breathed easy. She knew that was it. She watched Tre when he prepared the dope for burial. The sight of the package of dope spurred her on. She began to dig with a renewed vigor.

Finally Brianna excavated the package of dope, it was taped and double tapped, then wrapped in plastic, to protect it from the elements. She didn't even bother to brush off the leftover particles of dirt. She merely clutched the package to her chest and rush inside her house.

As she begin tearing open the package. She couldn't believe how many lives had been destroyed for this white powder. She also didn't realize the worth of what she had in her possession. There was so much tape to tear through she began to get tired all over again. She decided to put the packages in her closet until she could figure out what she would do next. Brianna knew she had to figure out how and who to move them too.

Buzz, buzz, buzz. Where is that sound coming from Brianna thought to herself. She looked over on Tre's nightstand to see his cell phone vibrating off the stand onto the floor. She hurried and picked the phone up. Looking at the outer display it read Jason. Brianna knew that Jason was one of Tre's out of town clientele. He was a southern hustler out of the ATL. She didn't know if the news had reached that far of Tre's death. So she decided to answer the phone.

"Hello."

"What Up Bri? Where Tre at?"

Hearing someone ask for Tre threw Brianna off, as she thought to herself he must not know.

"He's not here right now, I'll tell him you called Jason."

"Aight Bri, let him know I need to holla at him, a nigga dry down here."

"Ok I will let him know" with that Brianna hung up the phone, knowing that she had solved the problem of who, now it was just a matter of how.

ABOUT THE AUTHOR

Blake Karrington is an Essence Magazine® #1 Bestselling novelist. More than an author, he's a storyteller who places his readers in action-filled moments. It's in these creative spaces that readers are allowed to get to know his complex characters as if they're really alive.

Most of Blake's titles are centered in the South, in urban settings, that are often overlooked by the mainstream. But through Blake's eyes, readers quickly learn that places like Charlotte, NC can be as gritty as they come. It's in these streets of this oft overlooked world where Blake portrays murderers and thieves alike as believable characters. Without judgment, he weaves humanizing back stories that serve up compelling reasons for why one might choose a life of crime.

Readers of his work, speak of the roller coaster ride of emotions that ensues from feeling anger at empathetic characters who always seem to do the wrong thing at the right time, to keep the story moving forward.

In terms of setting, Blake's stories introduce his readers to spaces they may or may not be used to - streetscapes with unkept, cracked sidewalks where poverty prevails, times are depressed and people are broke and desperate. In Blake storytelling space, morality is so curved that rooting for bad guys to get away with murder can sometimes seem like the right thing for the reader to do - even when it's not. Readers who connect with Blake find him to be relatable.

Likening him to a bad-boy gone good, they see a storyteller who writes as if he's lived in the world's he generously shares, readily conveying his message that humanity is everywhere, especially in the unlikely, mean streets of cities like Charlotte.

ALSO BY BLAKE KARRINGTON

BLAKE KARRINGTON
COLLECTION

A Thug worth fighting for
Who can I run to
Faith & Trust 1 & 2
Baby please come home to me
Drunk on a thugs love 1&2
God forgives 1&2
Tears in the trap
The King of the south 1&2
Trapstar 1-3
Country girls 1-3
Single ladies 1-4
Confessions of an Urban author
Fallin for a hustler like me 1&2
Counterfeit love 1&2
Beard Gang chronicles 1-3
What kind of Man would I be
Thickums
All or nothing
Love, lies, and consequences
Scheming for love

Blake Karrington Collection

Made in the USA
Middletown, DE
05 January 2023

21405498R00086